S. J McCray

Life of Mary F. McCray

Born and Raised a Slave in the State of Kentucky

S. J McCray

Life of Mary F. McCray
Born and Raised a Slave in the State of Kentucky

ISBN/EAN: 9783337404574

Printed in Europe, USA, Canada, Australia, Japan

Cover: Foto ©Raphael Reischuk / pixelio.de

More available books at **www.hansebooks.com**

LIFE OF

MARY F. McCRAY.

❧ ❧ ❧ ❧

BORN AND RAISED A SLAVE IN THE

STATE OF KENTUCKY.

❧ ❧ ❧ ❧

BY HER HUSBAND AND SON.

❧ ❧ ❧ ❧

PREFACE.

❧ ❧ ❧

It is after much meditation and prayer that we undertake the task before us, for the reason that we feel keenly our inability to do justice in writing this book, the subject of which said many times during the last two years of her life that she believed that if the history of her life was written it would be a great blessing to many who are burdened down with the cares of this life, and who know nothing or little of Him who has said, ''Cast all your burdens on Me, for I care for you.'' For we can truly say that the subject of this sketch did know some things about the trials of this life, for she was born in the dark dark days of slavery, when there was not a ray of light for the freedom of the colored race. We hope that the reader will bear with us for speaking of the bondage of the colored race in this United States, as the subject was once a slave, and the enslavement of the colored race was a terrible curse on the American people. Our blessed Lord, in His own good time, said that they had suffered enough, so slavery was destroyed by a terrible war and the loss of many lives. But at the present time there is a greater curse on this nation than the enslavement of the colored race, that is, the awful curse of the liquor traffic, which touches every man, woman and child. Many volumes might be written on this terrible curse, but it would be impossible to begin to tell of the suffering it brings to the human family. We say sometimes, Oh, Lord, how long wilt thou let this go on?

The object in writing the life of this woman is not to make money, but it was her wish and desire, that it might be a great blessing to many readers, and to let them know what it is to live a holy, self-denial life amidst all the duties of this life, for she was a good woman and full of the Holy Ghost and of faith. She did much good to all wherever her lot was cast. Hoping that this work may prove as great a blessing to its readers as it has to its author and those who helped in composing its pages, we dedicate this photograph of a woman of God to all that love a pure, clean, complete, and full salvation, free from all sin to all people in every land.

CHAPTER I.

৵ ৵ ৵

BIRTH AND PARENTS OF SUBJECT.

Her father's name was Jonathan Taylor. He was born in Jefferson county, Kentucky. His master was his father, so that he was born free and did not serve as a slave. Her mother was born in old Hamilton county, of the same state. The date of their marriage could not be ascertained. To them were born sixteen children, fourteen girls and two boys, all destined to serve in slavery. Providentially, the owner of the subject's mother was an old maid. She was very good to her slave, and did not allow them to be abused, as were those belonging to many others. The subject's mother had all the care of her family herself, while her sister had all the clothes to make for all the rest of the slaves on the place. In addition she had much other work, which kept her busy every moment during the day and far into the night, so that she might earn a litttle money to buy her children some clothes to wear on Sunday. The holders did not make any provision for Sunday clothes for their slaves, but let them go any way, so that it was a hard and miserable life to live.

CHAPTER II.

❧ ❧ ❧

BIRTH OF SUBJECT AND HER CHILDHOOD DAYS.

The subject of this sketch was born May 26, 1837. She was the fifth child of the family, and was also the favorite child, as she was named after her mother. Her mother always said that she knew Fannie would get along well, as she was always ready to help her mother to do the work about the house, and loved to sow and knit and piece quilts. She had to do all this kind of work, and did it mostly at night, as all the slaves were obliged to work out on the plantation, men, women and children, from morning until night.

The subject was always an obedient and tender hearted child, always inclined to be religious. Whenever she heard of the death of any one, her first inquiry was, whether they had religion. She always thought that everybody who died must be converted, although she was not converted herself.

Her father was a great violin player, and taught his daughter how to dance, as he was a very wicked man, and her mother was a wicked woman. So there were none in her family to encourage her to seek the Lord. Consequently, she began to be hardened in sin, and learned to be quite a dancer, in common with the rest of the young people in that neighborhood. Her aunt was a good, Christian woman and was the first to speak to her about the salvation of her soul. Her aunt said to her one night while she was preparing to go to a ball, these words: "Fanny, when will you stop dancing? You will keep on until some of you will dance into hell." She answered: "Aunt Margaret (which was her aunt's name) this is my last time." Her aunt then said: "Fanny, you are not only promising this to me, but to the Lord also." The girl replied, "I did not know that the promise I made was to the Lord, too," and from that time on the words of her aunt followed her until she was under deep conviction for the pardon of her sins. She was then about fourteen years of age.

CHAPTER III.

❦ ❦ ❦ .

HER COMMISSION.

In those days there were no churches for the slaves on the plantation, but they were compelled to go from one plantation to another to hold their meetings in their log cabins. She used to go with her aunt and others to those prayer meetings. The mighty power of God would be in the meetings. They would hold their meetings sometimes nearly all night. Many would fall under the mighty power of God, and many of them would get soundly converted.

Our subject was greatly urged to seek the Lord. She went forward and soon found that she was a lost sinner without the blood of Jesus to wash away all her sins.

They would work hard all day in the corn fields and nearly every night would go two or three miles from home to attend meeting. Many were converted every night. She was somewhat discouraged because she was so slow to believe. Her cousin fell under the mighty power of God, and was happily converted, coming through shouting and praising God, and commenced at once to preach to the people, telling them to flee from the wrath to come. She said to our subject to believe and she would be converted. This encouraged her to go on.

She was trying to get converted shouting, like her cousin, but the Dear Lord did not come to her in that way. She did reason with the devil for some time, who told her that if she did not shout she would not have religion. She had a terrible struggle to get over that. After that terrible struggle about getting converted shouting, her faith was greatly increased, and while she was praying one day she was wonderfully blessed. She told her cousin how she felt. Her cousin told her that she had religion. She said, "Oh, no, I am just getting in a good way." She did not understand the scheme of the devil, so she was defeated and had to do her work all over again. But the Holy Spirit still strove with her. The meetings were still going on with increased power. She attended nearly ever night. The old people encouraged her, and then she began to take part in speaking and praying. By so doing the same blessing came to her again, but she was not satisfied. She went on in that state quite a long time. Finally one night she went to bed and fell into a dream, or trance, she did not know which. However, a man came to her while she was in that vision. She was trying to cross a clear stream of water. The man she believed to be a white man. He threw a narrow board in the middle of the stream of water, and there was also a broad board in the stream. The man told her to make her choice. She stepped on the narrow one and went across. As soon as she was across he showed her a beautiful place and told her it was heaven. She saw her cousin there and she was with all the angels. They were all just alike. She turned to come back, when she heard a voice saying: "You have just as much religion as those who shout." After that she woke up. She felt very strange and told her aunt about the vision. Her aunt said that she would

get through all right. In a short time afterwards she received
the witness of the Holy Spirit that her sins were all forgiven.
She was then a happy girl. She knew that her sins were all
washed away by the blood of Jesus. She could sing this song:

"Oh! happy day, that fixed my choice,
On Thee, my Savior and my God;
Well may this glowing heart rejoice,
And tell its rapture all abroad."
"Happy day! Happy day!
When Jesus washed my sins away.
He taught me how to watch and pray,
And live rejoicing every day,
Happy day! Happy day!
When Jesus washed my sins away."

The meeting spread from one plantation to another, and
many of the poor slaves' hearts were made to rejoice, for the
Lord Jesus visited them, notwithstanding they were treated
only as cattle and horses. Thanks be unto the Lord God of
Heaven, who did look down upon them in their helpless condition in tender mercy.

The subject of this sketch was a faithful young Christian,
laboring in the prayer meetings from house to house. They did
not have churches of their own. She related that one night
their prayer meeting continued until daylight, the power of
God having fallen upon the people in such a wonderful manner
that they fell on the floor like dead men and women. Many
of them had to go one, two and three miles to their homes, and
some of them were greatly punished for being away from their
houses at that late hour of night, for most all of them were

compelled to go to work before daylight. But in spite of all this cruel treatment they would pray and sing so that it would disturb their old masters so that they could not sleep and they would whip them, but still the poor slaves would continue to serve the Lord.

Our subject said that one of the masters in that part of Kentucky, a cruel slave holder whose name we can not recall, had a slave (a man) by the name of Dick, who was a true man of God. His master was so bitterly opposed to his serving the Lord as not to even permit him to return thanks at the table before taking his meals. But Dick had settled the matter, and the more his master would punish him the more he would pray for his master. At length his prevailing prayer with his God was the salvation of his master, and he was converted in a wonderful manner at a camp meeting. Dick was present, and his master ran to him, threw his arms around him and took him up and carried him around in the camp ground. After his conversion he set Dick free, and, giving him a horse, saddle and bridle, told him to go and preach the gospel everywhere. He also set free all the rest of his slaves. Oh, it is wonderful how God can use a man. This is true

CHAPTER IV.

❧ ❧ ❧

Our subject's associations were mostly among the old Christians, and her Christian life was far in advance of many of her elders. So much was this the case that some of the older Christians would tell her that she could live in that happy state of mind. She thought this very strange talk for the older Christians to tell to young converts, but it was her delight to serve the Lord. In her younger days she would work hard all day in the field with the rest of the field hands, and then would walk to a prayer meeting, should there chance to be one anywhere in the neighborhood. Frequently she would walk a distance of two or three miles. This song was her inspiring hope:

Oh, how happy are they who their Savior obey,
    And have laid up their treasures above.
Tongue can never express the sweet comfort and peace
    Of the soul in its earliest love.
That sweet comfort was mine when the favor divine
    I first found in the blood of the Lamb.
When my heart first believed, what a joy I received,
    What a heaven in Jesus' name.
Jesus all the day long was my joy and my song,
    Oh, that all His salvation might see.
He hath loved me, I cried, He has suffered and died,
    To redeem even rebels like me.

Her life was a life of joy in serving the Lord. Her mistress, who, as before stated, was an old maid, and very kind to her slaves. It was the custom among slave owners to hire a poor white man as overseer. Most all overseers were very cruel to the slaves in their charge. Our subject's mistress always had an overseer, but did not allow him to treat her slaves illy, so they were favored in the way of kind treatment above all the other slaves in the neighborhood in which she lived. Also some of the slaves might have had somewhat of an education had they wanted it, but not knowing that they ever would be free failed to take advantage of the opportunity. As slaves, they did not need an education. Slaves in those days did not know the words in a book, but they did know how to serve the Lord. Our subject's trial was as a Christian. Her mother was sick most of the time, and her mistress finally became impatient and offered her for sale to her father for the sum of fifty dollars. But he would not buy her, as he said he could have no use for slaves subject to ill health all the time. But had she been a healthy woman this man could not have bought her for less than five or six hundred dollars. Slave women always sold as high in price as men. Good able bodied slaves never sold for less than from six to nine hundred dollars. A good carpenter, blacksmith or bricklayer always sold for from one thousand to fifteen hundred dollars. The reader will have an idea from this how those poor human beings were bought and sold as horses and cattle.

Her mother had another very severe attack of sickness, worse than she had ever had, and the doctors said she must die. She was now under a very heavy burden. The thought that her mother might die without being consecrated brought her faith to a severe test, as she was only a young Christian. In these hours of trouble and bewilderment she called upon the Lord, as Jacob did in the days of old. She wrestled in prayer and expressed her thoughts to God for the salvation of her mother. Her prayers were answered. Her mother became suddenly converted and lived a long time afterward. She finally died triumphant in the faith of Christ and went home to glory. It was a very great trial for her to see her mother die and leave all of them behind. The youngest child was only three years old, but the dear Lord gave her grace to bear up under her burdens, all for His name's sake, for we know that He does all things for the best.

Her mother then being gone, all the responsibilities of the family fell upon her, as her father did not live on the same plantation with them. He only came home once a week, so that not much of the family cares could rest upon him. She had to fill the place in the household which her mother had occupied, as her sister did not take much interest in the care of the children. She was the only one in the family who was a Christian. From this she learned much about the strong arm of the Lord, who has promised to be with us six hours, and in the seventh He will not forsake us. Oh, how we ought to praise God for His wonderful saving grace.

CHAPTER VI.

❧ ❧ ❧

THE DEATH OF HER MISTRESS.

Our subject's mistress died in the year A. D. 1859. She stated in her will that all her relations, each and every one, should have a share in her estate. Then her slaves were to be set free and a certain sum of money was set apart to bring them to the state of Ohio, and also enough money to buy eighty acres of land for each of the two families. Our subject's father's family was one of the two, and her mother's sister's family was the other. The name of the sister was Margaret Taylor. Most all the slaves of the mistress was embraced in those two families. A short time after her estate was settled, some of her relations were enraged because Aunt Polly Adams, as they called her, had set her slaves free. So some of them began at once an attempt to break the will. Miss Polly Adams was never a married lady. She had made two wills, and it was the last one that contained the provisions for the freedom of her slaves and their removal to Ohio. However her relations kept the slaves there for three years while they were trying to break the will. One complaint was that Miss Polly had willed real estate to her slaves. Their lawyers informed them that it was useless for them to complain, as the will could never be broken. Then the freed slaves were told to go to the place assigned to them. They were not long in getting to this place, as they were only three miles from the Ohio river. They took the steamer at a place called Hannily's Landing for Cincinnati. After their arrival in that city they met a gentleman who had been notified of three colored people who had just arrived from the South and was ready to take care of them. The writer can truly say that Mr. Coffin was a true friend indeed to colored people. For many years he was the leading man of the city, and helped many poor slaves from the land of bondage to the land of freedom.

In the dark days of slavery, when the black laws of the United States was in force, which carried a penalty of five hundred dollars fine and several years in the penitentiary for any person that would assist a slave to escape from bondage to freedom, the writer can say that many white men of the northern states gave up their property, yes, and some of them their lives, in rescuing poor slaves from their bondage. Mr. Levi Coffin stood at the head of his followers in this noble work of rescuing slaves that came into the city of Cincinnati. This man's house was the union depot of all underground railways.

It may be better to explain what is meant by the underground railway. It means that white men organized themselves into a body to help those poor slaves who had energy and perseverance enough to run away from bondage and seek a land of liberty. They would establish stations a number of miles apart, generally at the house of one of the members. They would conceal the slaves who chanced to be under their protection during the daytime, but as soon as the shades of night began to fall the slaves were placed in covered wagons and taken, concealed as freight, to another one of the stations. This process was kept up until they reached the union depot, and then they were transferred into Canada, this being the only place where runaway slaves were sure of a safe refuge. Hundreds sought their freedom in this manner.

The writer can say that the colored people were subjected to a great deal of abuse and ill treatment at the hands of the white people of the North, not because they were less worthy of respect than any other people, but simply because their faces were black. The story of the terrible suffering of the colored people of the South at the close of the war has never yet been printed. Many of the rebels would mask themselves and amuse themselves by horse-whipping the poor slaves. Yes, and even assassinate them, taking the lives of whole families. These crimes continued for years, but those cruel days have been washed away by the tide of time, never to return again.

It has been said that our race of people can never stand on a level with the whites, but we candidly deny that statement. The white race has been more than five thousand years climbing the ladder of fame, while the colored race has only had opportunities for improvement for about two hundred years. But in the last twenty-five years the progress of the Negro race has been wonderful. We believe that had proper steps been taken and careful observations made of the condition of affairs in the South at the close of the war, the Negro race would be seventy years in advance of the position it occupies to-day. The bloody war resulted in envy, hatred, strife, malice and prejudice between the black and the white, which is sin of the worst nature. There was no kind of brotherly love shown, but, rather, man's inhumanity to man, which has caused countless thousands to mourn. Christ teaches us to love one another, and nothing but the blood of Christ can remedy this condition and save people from all evil.

CHAPTER VII.

❧ ❧ ❧

THE PURCHASE OF LAND FOR THE TAYLOR FAMILY.

Mr. Coffin took charge of the two families of Taylors. That was also the name of the husband of the aunt of our subject, although he was no relative to her father. Mr. Coffin looked out for a location for the families, and succeeded in renting two large houses, in which they began to keep house. In the family of which our subject was a member there were no boys, the two born into the family having died when quite young. Consequently the large girls had to do all the hard work. Some of them went to work in private families.

They remained in the city quite a long time, but at least Mr. Coffin went to Mercer county, Ohio, to buy them a farm with the money left them by their mistress. This was sufficient to buy them one hundred and sixty acres of good land. It took him some time to bargain for a farm, but he finally succeeded, having purchased one that was well timbered. He then returned to the city and reported his success. It was then

some time before they could move, as there were no railroads
in that country in those days, the only way of transportation
being the canal. They packed their goods and started on a
canal boat for their new home. This mode of travel was very
poor, as compared with the quick transportation of the present
day, as the boats were drawn by mules or horses, and hence but
slow progress was made. At length, however, at the end of
thirteen days they arrived at New Bremen, Mercer county,
Ohio, their farm being about twelve miles from that place.
The neighbors in that settlement kindly consented to let them
have the use of their teams with which to remove their goods to
their farm.

On each of the farms there was a log cabin. Each farm contained eighty acres, and our subject moved onto the west
eighty, of which there was only a few acres cleared. She had
no brothers to assist her father in the heavy work, such as chopping down the heavy timber, splitting rails, and clearing off
the land in general to get it ready for farming. Her father
knew very little about farming, and as before stated the cares
of the family rested very lightly upon him. For this reason it
was very hard for them to get along well. Worse than all,
everybody in the neighborhood were in about the same condition, so they could receive no help. Things looked very dark
and gloomy for them, and especially just after the close of the
civil war, when prices on all commodities were so high. There
was but little land cleared in all the neighborhood on which to
raise anything to sell. The only escape her father had was to
cut down his best oak timber and saw it into blocks, in which
shape it was sold for making barrels, kegs and other wood ves-
sels. Many farmers did great damage to their farms by cut-

ting their oak timber so soon. Many of them had three or four boys and the farms were cleared in a short time. In the family of our subject, however, there was no one who understood this kind of work, her father having been a distiller by occupation. We are sorry to say that while engaged in this sort of work the appetite for strong drink fascinated him, and found him intoxicated many times and brought home in that condition. To his credit be it said that he never abused his family, as is the case with so many drinking men while under the influence of liquor.

Our subject was compelled to take almost entire charge of the family, to be, so to speak, father, mother and sister all at the same time. She would help her father, who was of a delicate constitution, at much of his hard work. Sometimes they would hire a man to help at this. She would even chop wood and help load it on wagons. This she had to do in order to earn enough money to procure the necessities of life. Many a time she would be at her wit's end to know what to do in order to keep the family from want, and scarcely knew what to do. But she knew there was One who would not forsake her, so she called upon the Lord, who has said, "In the days of trouble I will deliver thee," and we can say that our blessed Lord did help her in the time of need.

CHAPTER VIII.

✳ ✳ ✳

FARM LIFE CONTINUES.

The farm life continued with increased trials and burdens. Her father was at length confined to his bed from receiving a bad injury to one of his limbs. He was not able to do any work for six months or more. Many doctors were consulted, but none could give him relief. The neighbors were very kind to her, and helped her in many ways during her father's affliction. This was a great trial for her, one of the greatest she was ever called upon to endure, but she did not forget to cast her burdens upon One who has said, "Cast all your burdens upon Me, for I care for you." There were also many precious promises in the Bible, such as: "I will never leave thee, nor forsake thee," and "Call upon me in the days of trouble and I will deliver thee in due time."

One day a young doctor by the name of Thomas was passing through the neighborhood. He had the reputation of being a very skillful physician, and she went to see him. She told him of the condition of her father, and the doctor made her some salve and told her how to use it on her father's limb. She went home and began to do as the doctor had directed and in a short time her father was once more able to breath fresh

air, to work and help care for his family. Then affairs moved
along very well, but in the same old channel, and with but
little prospects for improvement in the way of monetary matters. Some of her sisters became very much discouraged because of the hard times they had in getting along, and three of
them went back to Cincinnati to work by the week, agreeing to
send money back to assist in helping support the rest of the
family. Thus was a great strain lifted from the family, and it
was a great help, too, as the three girls did as they had agreed.
Yet our subject had hard trials. She was the life of the family,
and, with all, the only Christian in this large family of girls.
This caused her to realize that she must let her light shine as
a Christian in the home before her sisters and father.

Christianity had but few adherents in the neighborhood
surrounding her home, either among the old or young. Her
mind would often turn to her former experiences as a Christian.
This would cause her to realize that she had lost much of the
joy of the Lord out of her soul. Often, when she would go out
among the young people and see many of them who professed
to be Christians enjoying themselves among the sinners, the
devil would tempt her, saying: "Why don't you enjoy your-
self like the other young people; they profess to be Christians
as well as you." But she could never do like the rest of them,
for she knew what great things God had done for her in these
trials and temptations, and she called upon Him to give her
grace so that she might not yield to the devil and take part in
the outbroken sins like some of the old and young about her,
many of whom professed to be Christians, but who were merely
using Christianity as a cloak to protect them in the service of
the devil. The Omnipotent One watched with His tender

mercies over her, and gave her the utmost strength and grace to endure such vital temptations, and to let her light shine so that all men might see her good works in the vineyard of our Lord.

CHAPTER IX.

✤ ✤ ✤

DEATH OF HER SISTER, SIDNEY ANN.

Our Savior said in His blessed word, that in this world ye shall have trials and tribulations, but in peace. Sidney Ann went to a neighboring town to work, where she had been for about a month when she caught a severe cold that settled on her lungs. This weakened her so that she was unable to work, and in consequence went home, where she soon took to her bed. She was tenderly waited on and everything was done that might relieve her from her sufferings. But nothing did her much good and it was thought that she must die. Our subject thought that her sister was living a sinful life and was not prepared to meet her God. Sidney Ann was told that she could not recovor, and our subject earnestly beseeched the Lord to have mercy on her sister and save her from her sins. At the same time she told her sister she must pray for herself. Our subject gave herself much to prayer. She also called on some of the neighbors to come in and help pray for her sister, that she might awaken to a sense of her lost condition. She still continued to pray by day and by night that her prayers in behalf of her dying sister might be answered. The neighbors called frequently and much prayer was offered up to the Lord. Finally, her sister awoke and said that she was a lost soul, without the blood of Jesus might be applied to her heart to wash away her sins and cleanse her from all unrighteousness. She then began to pray, cry and scream for mercy. Our subject's faith was strengthened to see her sister break down and pray for the Lord to forgive her and make her pure and holy before she died. Our subject said that the dear Lord, in His tender mercies, did come to her sister's heart, and broke the bands of unbelief and allowed her poor captive soul to go free. At last the cloud of darkness was dispelled from her soul, and nothing but light, joy and gladness broke forth in superabundance from the soul that once was darkened in sin, and now she could sing.

"On Christ the solid rock I stand,
All other ground is sinking sand."

Our subject's heart was made to leap with joy and gladness when she saw her sister so filled with the presence and power of the Lord Jesus. Though she did not live long to tell the beautiful story of Christ, yet she lost no opportunity in telling every one who came to see her. She lived only four months after she was taken ill. In full triumph of living faith she went sweeping through the gates of that eternal city whose streets are paved with gold, that city where life is everlasting, and where we see our departed ones. Our subject was now greatly encouraged, more than ever before, to live the life of the righteous. Oh, what a mistake mankind is making in delaying to seek the Lord for the salvation of their souls until they are upon the bed of death. Thousands and thousands miss heaven by so doing. Even should any be saved at that late hour they must go, as did our sister, empty handed into the presence of the Master, and without a star in their crowns. Oh, dear reader, do not wait, for the blessed word says: "To-day is the day of salvation."

CHAPTER X.

❧ ❧ ❧

SPIRITUAL CONDITION OF PEOPLE IN THE NEIGHBORHOOD.

The spiritual condition of the people in the neighborhood at that time was very poor. There were three churches, two Methodist and one Baptist, all situated very close to each other. The members of these churches did not think much about serving the Lord. Most of them, both old and young, were leaders in play parties that met from house to house, and one devil could watch them, as they were not engaged in the service of the Lord. The principal amusement at these parties was dancing, and many of the older members would take active part with the younger people in that kind of sport and fun.

Our subject would sometimes yield to the temptation and go and look on. While she was doing this the tempter would whisper in her ear: "Why are you looking so sanctimonious? These young people are all Christians, and so are the older ones. Why do you not take part with them? You are no better than they." She would answer within herself, that is so. The writer will say that at times a converted person will be tempted to listen to the tempter and desire worldly pleasure. The devil will say that it matters not. If you have the word of God in your heart that should not keep you from having a little worldly pleasure. Other professors of religion do the very same things and why not you? There are many truly converted souls that have not had the proper teaching in the early part of their Christian experience. They should be taught how to resist the devil and keep from yielding to him, and to shun worldly enjoyments. But if these rules are not followed out the Lord will depart from them, and, step by step, the adversary will lead them on and on, testifying for the Lord when they are in utter darkness, and perhaps have been for weeks and months, in their wild excitement.

At the dancing parties some of the younger ones would try to persuade our subject to join them in dancing. When the music would start it was a very strong temptation to resist dancing after music having been of her greatest enjoyments before her conversion. In those moments of temptation the Lord would give her grace to resist the devil.

There are thousands and thousands of professors in the churches to-day who take part in worldly enjoyments, and know nothing of the spirit of the Lord. Many of these were once happily converted. The great cause of so much backsliding is that we have not ministers and leaders who are living up to their professions. They have lost the realization of the spirit of Christ, and therefore, they can not lead the young souls into fountains of living waters. We all know that it is impossible for the blind to lead the blind, as they will both fall. So both preacher and members drift along the broad path that leads to death eternal night. Oh, what a fearful responsibility rests upon a pastor who says he is called to preach the gospel to dying men and women. Oh, may the dear Lord wake up these dead souls that are sleeping on and will not be awakened, because they pay their pastors big salaries to let them sleep on in their sins. They think they are saved because they are members of the church and pay the preacher his dues. But in that great judgment day they will hear the woeful cry, "Depart from Me, ye churches, into the lake of everlasting burning, prepared for the devil and his angels."

CHAPTER XI.

ANOTHER SISTER NIPPED BY THE FROST OF TIME.

It was scarcely a year after the death of Sidney Ann before another sister was taken with the same complaint. A heavy cold settled on her lungs and nothing could be done for her, as it speedily developed into quick consumption, which dreadful disease can not be cured. Sarah, like the other sister, had no hope in Christ, and now, upon her dying bed, must seek salvation for her poor immortal soul, at an hour almost too late. Our subject saw that no time was to be lost, and so, as heretofore, she prayed that God might save her sister, as it would not do for her to pass away without eternal life. The sister, like the other one, was hard to believe, but finally she gave up all to him who has said: "Son, or daughter, the day thou givest Me thine heart I will be fond of thee," and, with one mighty act of living faith in the all-obtaining blood of the Lord Jesus, the great burden of sin was rolled from her heart and her soul was filled with joy and peace. She died shortly after her conversion in the full triumph of living faith, but met her Savior empty handed. Oh, how good and blessed is the Lord Jesus, who allows us to live through all our sins and when the time arrives for us to die saves us from our iniquities. This is evidence that God has promised to answer the prayers of His dear children who pray to Him by day and by night. It is wonderful how God allows mankind to live in their sins, until death stares them in the face, and then saves them.

To all those who may read this book, the writer wishes to say: Do not do as this young woman did. The devil will no doubt try you while you are reading this book, and whisper to you that you can be converted on your death bed, but the blessed book says: "To-day is the day of salvation." See at once, dear reader, that the word of your God does not come into contact with the evil suggestings of the devil. The devil suggests to thousands that they wait until they are on a sick bed before seeking the Lord. He also suggests the same thing to many believers, telling them that they need not pray and talk so much about living a holy life, as there will be plenty of time to attend to that after they are taken down sick. Thousands of poor souls are thus deceived and take refuge in the devil. Often their lives are cut off without warning, and many are thus cast into the lake of everlasting fire. Oh, may our blessed Lord assist the millions of souls who are waiting for repentance upon the death bed to make up their minds at once to serve Him.

Our subject lifted up her heart in praise unto the Lord for helping her to bear up under the great trial of burying two of her sisters within one year. With all the care of the family bearing heavily upon her, the Lord lent her a helping hand, and gave her strength to endure the trials. While living in the country our subject became quite familiar with the ways of the Northern people. She found great difference between them and the slaves in the South. The slaves had no work to manage or plan for. There was always some one to do the planning and buying and selling for them. In the North she had all this to do for herself, in addition to the care of the family. Her father cared very little about business, and he would allow some of the neighbors to take advantage of him. He was kind-hearted and would not have trouble with anyone, even if he was getting the worst of the bargain. So our subject had to spend most of her time in transacting the business of the farm. Her father thought every one was honest like himself. He always carried the motto, "Honesty is the best policy," stamped in his heart. At one time he was swindled very badly by one of his neighbors, a man that owned a saw mill, and who was buying all the timber he could get, especially oak and walnut, which were very valuable and commanded a high price. This mill owner had the reputation of being a very dishonest man, and would get the better of all who transacted business with him if possible, and her father was no exception. He hauled timber enough to build a new house, and when he went for the lumber prepared from his logs he found that the mill owner had exchanged poor lumber for the fine logs he had taken there. When our subject saw how her father had been swindled, she resolved that it was to the interest of the family for her to take more interest in the buying and selling.

CHAPTER XII.

OUR SUBJECT LEAVES HOME TO WORK.

Finally the family became so greatly in need of clothing that it became necessary for our subject to go from home to work and earn money. Some of the other sisters had worked away from home, but they did not help the family as much as they should have done. They had the interests of the family very little at heart, and spent their money on themselves. So there was no way for her to do but to earn the needed money. There was no place in the neighborhood to work, as the settlers were all poor like herself. She told her father that she must go to some town to earn money to buy them some clothing, as their supply was nearly gone. Her father said he did not see how he could get along without her. But she told him that she must go, as he could get but very little work to do. After making all necessary preparations, in company with her sister Charlotte and a cousin, she was soon on her way to Lima, Ohio, about forty miles from home. They had to work most all the way, as they had no money. They had taken only a few things with them. It was a long journey for these three young women to make without any one to accompany and guide them. Our subject knew something about the help of the Lord, therefore she trusted in Him to protect her from any harm or danger. They were very prosperous in their first day's journey, and after walking thirty miles, a kind friend took them in, gave them plenty to eat and shelter for the night. The next morning they were very much refreshed, but did not get a very early start, as they had only a little over twelve miles to go.

They arrived in Lima early in the afternoon of the second day, and found a stopping place at the home of Mrs. ———, who was kind enough to keep them two or three days until they could find places to work. Within a week her sister found a place in a private family, as did her cousin also. As for herself, Mrs. ——— thought she could earn more in working by the day, so, making Mrs. ———'s house her headquarters, assisting her when she had no work elsewhere, she did a great deal of work for other people. She stayed with Mrs. ——— a long time, but at length she discovered that Mrs. ——— did not do right. Many things caused her pain, but she bore it as long as she thought best. She found out so many tricks this woman was capable of and yet she claimed to be a member of the church. An instance of the manner in which she was treated. At one time Mrs. ——— concealed a silver thimble and charged her with stealing it. This seemed to be a very severe charge to make against one who was a perfect stranger, and it was all she could do to endure it. She was conscious of the fact, however, that her God knew she was not a thief. She assisted Mrs. ——— in searching all over the house for the lost thimble, but it could not be found, at length she told Mrs. ——— that she would pay for it, but she answered she was not worrying about her paying for it, but the trouble was to clear herself of the charge of theft. She was at her wit's end, but remembering the words of her blessed Master, " Call upon Me in the days of thy trouble, and I will deliver thee," she decided to bide her time. She paid Mrs. ——— for the thimble. Not long afterwards she was sweeping and dusting two or three rooms in the house, and while placing everything in its proper place she found the thimble. She called Mrs. ——— and told her that she had found the lost thimble, but received the reply that she was the possessor of two thimbles. It so happened that a minister was boarding at the house. He overheard the conversation, and, stepping into the room, told Mrs. ——— that he had heard her accuse several other girls in regard to that thimble. He then spoke to her of the way she was treating our subject by accusing her of stealing. At this Mrs. ——— cried and went out of the room, leaving our subject to finish her work of cleaning the house. She felt in her heart that she was cleared of the charge of stealing the thimble, and that it was through the help of the dear Lord that her deliverance had come. It is a very distressing thing to be caught in a lie. Afterward, Mrs. ———'s next door neighbor told how she had told lies about her, and about the minister also, and of the things Mrs. ——— had stolen from her boarders and other people who came about the house.

Our subject did not have any confidence in Mrs. ——— as one claiming to be a Christian. Though acquainted with the character of Mrs. ——— our subject still remained in her house. Soon after the trouble about the thimble a lady wanted our subject to do some work for her. Not having the money to pay she offered a good second hand carpet in payment. Our subject agreed to do the work for the carpet. It was a rag carpet and would be of good service on the farm. While our subject was working for another lady, Mrs. ———, who was acquainted with the lady that had the carpet, told her that she would do the work and take the carpet as pay, but the lady answered that she had engaged Mary Taylor to do the work. Mrs. ——— stated that Mary Taylor did not want the carpet. The lady did not know what to think about Mrs. ———'s statement, as there had been no time set when our subject should do the work. The lady did not know what to do, so she said: "If Mary does not want the carpet you may do the work," and adding, "but I do not know why Mary should change her mind in regard to it." The lady felt that something was wrong, but allowed Mrs. ——— to do the work, and our subject had no knowledge that it had been performed. At length, having some spare time she decided to do the work and get the carpet. She arrived at the house and was much surprised when the lady told her that she had been told that she did not want the carpet. Our subject asked the name of the party who made the statement and was told that it was Mrs.

——. She answered that she had never spoken to Mrs.
—— about the carpet. When she asked Mrs. —— about
the matter she answered that she did not think our subject had
any use for the carpet. She refused to have any trouble about
the carpet but now saw how Mrs. —— had told another
falsehood to cheat her out of the carpet. All her troubles
proved to be a blessing, however, to her as a follower of the
Lord Jesus, who said in His blessed word that "All things
work together for good to those who love and serve Him." She
now saw that it was not best to stay longer with Mrs. ——.
She found another home with a near neighbor by the name of
Mrs. Harris, who was very kind to her and permitted her to
make the house her home while she worked out by the day.
She only remained here long enough to fulfill all her engage-
ments, when she began to prepare to return home. Her stay
in Lima had been quite profitable, and in addition to a nice
little sum of money, she carried with her a number of articles
of clothing and household goods received in exchange for her
labor, for all of which she returned thanks to our dear Lord for
His love and kindness toward her.

CHAPTER XIII.

She arrived at her home and found her father and sisters

all very well. As soon as she had rested she began to look after the work, as usual, both in the house and on the farm. Everything was now moving along very well. The money she had earned while away from home was of great use to her father and sisters. It may now be seen more than ever the great part she took in managing the family affairs. Indeed her share was greater than the work performed by her mother, who had only a family and a house to look after, while she not only filled her mother's place in the home, but her father's place on the farm, also. At this time she was about twenty-four years of age and was strong and usually had good health.

CHAPTER XIV.

ANOTHER SISTER NIPPED BY THE FROST OF TIME.

About a year and a half after the death of her sister Sarah, another sister, Martha, was taken sick very suddenly with a heavy cold, like her other two sisters. They began at once to give Martha treatment, and in four or five weeks she began to grow better and continued to improve until she was able to go about the house. Our subject thought she was so much better that it would be safe to leave her in the care of her father and other sisters, as she had some work that called her away from home. She told her father that while she was gone he must take good care of Martha, and not allow her to go out of doors. After our subject had gone Martha continued to feel better and was getting along nicely. While she was away Martha concluded she felt well enough to go to a party, and decided to attend one given in the neighborhood. Our subject did not want Martha to go, fearing that she might take cold, but Martha, like all young girls, who are not truly Christians, love to go where there is fun and frolic, no matter what anyone might say. In going and coming from the party she got her feet wet and was again taken down sick. Everything was done to save her, but to no avail and she must die, praying on her death bed and with no hope for eternal life. Our subject remembered the words of the thief on the cross: "Lord, when Thou comest into Thy kingdom, remember me." The Lord said: "This day thou shalt be with Me." She told Martha that she must pray and call on the Lord to have mercy, and she sang and prayed with her sister, for she knew the Lord would hear and answer prayer. She had prevailed with God in prayer for her other sisters. She called in a few of the neighbors to sing and pray with her for the conversion of her sister. They had a good meeting, and when Martha was in earnest prayer the neighbors returned home. Our subject continued praying for her sister for several days and nights, and one day while she was singing one of her favorite hymns Martha was earnestly pleading with the Lord to have mercy upon her and forgive her of all her sins. Our subject continued singing the hymn and suddenly Martha let go of all the things of time and by faith took hold of the promise of God, which says: "Thy sins which are many are all forgiven thee." She felt that the great burden of sin had rolled away and her soul was filled with light, peace, joy and gladness. She said in a loud voice: "O, praise the Lord for the joy and peace which now fills my soul." Her father said, "Francis you are getting that girl excited," but Martha said, "O, no, father, I am not excited, the Lord has forgiven me of my sins." Our subject and Martha then had a good time praising the Lord. Martha only lived a short time afterward, but she spent most of the time exhorting and warning others not to do as she had done. She died in full faith, and went sweeping through the open gate into that eternal city. But she went empty handed, as thousands of other people are going every day. The writer warns the reader, "Do not wait for to-morrow," for the Lord says: "Behold this day is the day of salvation." Our subject was now more than ever encouraged to press on in the Christian life, so helpful in the presence of sickness and death.

CHAPTER XV.

❧ ❧ ❧

There was a great revival in the neighborhood, and all the churches and the three churches in the vicinity united in union meetings. Meetings were held first in the A. M. E. and then in the Baptist church. The meeting commenced in November, 1866 and closed in June, 1867. It was the greatest revival ever held in that part of the State of Ohio, before or since that time. A great number were converted during the continuation of the meeting, and many were called to preach the gospel. Some people who did not take part in the meeting predicted that the corn crop would be small, because the greater number of the people were constant in their attendance at the meeting. But, to their astonishment, there were better crops that year than ever before. The writer adds: "When people serve the Lord everything goes well."

CHAPTER XVI.

ᴥ ᴥ ᴥ

The writer became acquainted with the Taylor family in the year 1865. In the fall of that year I came home from the army to Cincinnati, then my home, and became acquainted with three of the sisters, two of whom were single, the other being married. The married sister lived in the same house where I was stopping. The family with whom I was boarding occupying a portion of the house. The two single sisters came to visit with their married sister. The younger of the unmarried sisters I only met a few times, but myself and the other two soon became great friends. At that time I had no thought of getting married. But about six months after the younger of the sisters mentioned above had returned to her home in Mercer county, I wrote her a letter, asking the privilege of writing to her as a friend, merely to pass away the time. She gave her consent and a correspondence was kept up for about nine months. During that time I sent her one of my pictures. I did not say anything about marrying, and in a short time we stopped writing to each other. I remained in Cincinnati for about one year, when my health became impaired by reason of attendance on a sick man. The doctor said that I had better go west. I waited for three months and not getting any better, in the spring of 1867, I went to the southwestern part of Michigan. I left Cincinnati on the first day of April and arrived at Cassapolis next day. I had to go about eight miles into the country to the home of an old army friend, where I was kindly welcomed. We were both very glad to meet again. Good farm hands were worth from $20 to $25 per month, but I was not experienced in farm work. After having had a good visit, my old friend, Joseph Cross, said that he had bought forty acres of land in the woods, and that he had sold one hundred cords of wood to a man who owned a woolen mill near the west end of his land. He said he would give me work of chopping the wood if I cared to do so. I had done but little chopping, but he offered me eighty-seven and a half cents per cord, and I accepted his offer. I began the work about the middle of April and finished it the last of June. I remained in the neighborhood a few days afterwards and then took my departure for Chicago. I was not there long before hearing that the captain of my company was in the city. I hunted him up, and he was very glad to see me. I was there a week before securing any work. At length I secured a place to work in a livery stable. I did not like that kind of employment and only remained there two months, when I secured a place to work in a private family.

CHAPTER XVII.

❧ ❧ ❧

My first letter of friendship to the subject of this sketch was dated August 1st, 1867. We had never seen each other, but we continued to write during the entire time I remained in Chicago. In 1868 I left Chicago and went to Mendota, Ill., where an old army comrade lived, whom I had not seen since we were mustered out of the service at Detroit in October, 1865. I visited with him until March, and when the spring work began to open up, my friend Hunter said he would assist me in finding some work. Hearing of a lady by the name of Mrs. Dr. Tud, who owned a farm about one mile out of the city, and that she wished to hire a man to work for nine months, Mr. Hunter went to see her with me. I was fortunate in securing the position for nine months at twenty dollars a month. I commenced work on the 15th of March and worked until October 15th, at which time my contract expired. She paid me and I then made my home at an aunt of Mr. Hunter's. She had no children, was a good Christian woman, and I had a nice home with her. Her husband was not a Christian, and neither was I, though I had not many bad habits, such as drinking strong drinks, swearing, smoking cigars, chewing tobacco, and keeping company with vile young people. But after all I knew I was a sinner and in order to become a Christian I must be converted. The Bible says every one must be born again, or they cannot enter the Kingdom of God.

The woman with whom I was boarding was a great help to me. Before I had seen her she had written Christian letters to Mr. Hunter and myself, while we were together in the same company on the field of battle and sleeping together in the same tent. I then began to think that I ought to become a Christian. There were only thirty or forty colored people, of whom part were Methodists and part Baptists. The latter had a house of worship, while the Methodists met in a little school house. In the early part of January, 1868, the Methodists held a revival in their regular place of meeting—the school house. They invited the Baptists to come in with them and hold union meetings. The meetings were held two weeks, with only one conversion. I was the one convert, for I had been seeking religion for a long time before their meeting began. I shall praise through all eternity for the pardon of my sins. I had a terrible struggle to get loose from the devil, because I was so full of unbelief, but one mighty look by faith to the all-atoning blood of Jesus, and the power of sin was broken and my captive soul set free. Oh! what joy and peace and gladness filled my soul. I know what it is to have the light of God in my soul. Before I was converted I did not know anything about the Bible, and I could not read it. I began the Christian life without any knowledge of reading God's word. My great desire was to have a Bible and learn to read it. I went to see Mrs. Tud, and told her what the Lord had done for me and how glad I would be to learn to read the Bible. She said she was a member of the Bible society, and she would give me a Bible. She gave me a large sized one, and I began to spell the words and read as well as I could as I advanced in Christian life. I became more and more hungry for Bible knowledge. I can truly say it was a wonder to me how the Lord helped me and opened my understanding to read His blessed word.

CHAPTER XVIII.

❧ ❧ ❧

COURTSHIP AND MARRIAGE.

My first letter of courtship to our subject was accepted. Our marriage was very strange indeed, and a surprise to both of us. There had been but little courting, and that had been done by correspondence. There was no positive engagement, nor was there any date fixed for our marriage. I do say to the readers of this narrative, who believe in the Lord and His guidance and who love and serve Him in all things, that the hand of the Lord was in this marriage. I wrote my last letter to her, stating that I would be at home in the fall, according to my promise. I left Mendota in October on the C., B. & Q. railroad. I arrived in Chicago and remained there twenty-four hours, leaving there on the Michigan Central railroad for Detroit. From there I went to Toledo and then to Lima, where I found the two sisters I had met four years previously while they were living in Cincinnati. The next day I wrote a a few lines to our subject, stating that I was in Lima and would wait to hear from her before leaving. In two weeks I received a letter from her saying that she would send a friend to meet me at New Bremen, providing I would write and let her know what day I would leave Lima. As soon as I received the letter I read and answered it at once, telling her on what day I would leave. In a day or two I began to prepare to start, and on the 16th day of November, late in the afternoon, I arrived in New Bremen. The friend was there to meet me. He introduced himself as Mr. Clark, and told me he had twelve miles to drive. I told him I had a trunk at the hotel. Hitching his horse to the wagon he drove after it. It was about four o'clock before we started. Mr. Clark had a good team of horses and by half past seven we were at his home. Mr. Clark's grandson took charge of the team and we went to into the house, where arrangements had been made for me to stay over night. Mr. and Mrs. Clark were our subject's best friends in the neighborhood. After a good night's rest and a good breakfast and dinner the next day we started for the home of our subject, which was a mile distant. When we arrived our subject was not at home. She was just across the field at her aunt's, but saw us coming and returned at once. Mr. Clark introduced me to her, for it was the first time I had seen her. I had not even seen her picture, but she had seen one of mine. Mr. Clark returned to his home and we spent a pleasant afternoon together. Toward the close I asked her a direct question—was she ready to marry me? She said yes. I asked her when and she said, " to-morrow night." She said that Mr. Clark would take me to Celina to get the license. I bade her good afternoon. As I left the house I met her father and introduced myself to him. He said he had heard his children talking about me. I asked him about marrying his daughter. He said he had no objections, so that everything was all right. Early next morning Mr. Clark started for Celina, accompanied by myself, to get the license.

We returned late in the afternoon. The whole affair had been kept secret, none but Mr. Clark and his family knowing of it until we returned with the license, when several friends and neighbors were invited to attend the wedding. At about eight o'clock the same evening we were united in marriage. It was the greatest surprise that ever happened in that neighborhood. I wish to add that had I gone to see my wife every day for five years before our marriage I could not have succeeded in getting a better one. Neither would an engagement of six months duration added to her good qualities. Were she alive I feel sure she would make the samestatement regarding me as her husband. I can truly say that our married life was a happy one, as both of us were Christians—not formal church members, as are many of to-day who simply join the church without experiencing conversion. This was not so with us. My wife was converted when she was about fifteen years old and my conversion occurred about a year before our marriage. Thus, we were prepared to make each other happy, not only in this life, but to help each other live the life of the righteous. It has been said: "True happiness does not consist of the things on this world, but in the meek and quiet spirit which should dwell in the soul of every true Christian, which is true happiness."

CHAPTER XIX.

ᴥ ᴥ ᴥ

Mr. and Mrs. Clark gave us a very fine wedding supper. Mrs. Clark did the cooking, and she was an expert. A large number of guests were there, both married people and single. All who were invited came, and everything was favorable to a pleasant occasion. It was in the latter part of the month of November, and the evening was very nice, just cool enough to make it pleasant. All came early in order that a social talk might be had before supper. Of course the bride was the topic of conversation during the evening, although the groom came in for his full share. Mrs. Clark sent word that supper was ready, and as many as were required to fill the first table quickly responded. The bride and groom occupied seats of honor at the head of the table. The table was spread with everything good to eat, and plenty 'for all. Soon after supper many returned home, wishing the bride and groom all possible success in life. After all had returned we remained a short time with Mrs. Clark. About eleven o'clock we returned home, and the wedding festivities were at an end.

We were soon to be left alone, as all of my wife's sisters had left home and her father was preparing to return to Kentucky. We talked and planned for the future, and debated whether it would be best to remain on the farm or not. Each of the sisters had equal shares in the farm, and the property was in bad condition. There was only one horse and it was not suitable for the work required, and there was very little else to do with. There was no grain for seed and a very little for bread. Only twenty-five acres of the farm had been cleared, and the only thing on the farm that gave any promise of prosperity were two milch cows. There was no encouragement to remain. After considering everything I told my wife that it was useless to invest any money in the farm, for if we did we might have trouble with the other girls and their husbands, and that the best thing to do was to leave. She did not want to do this, but I insisted that it was the only thing for us to do, and then the matter was dropped. Often afterwards the question as to what was best to do came up for discussion. At last she said if a farm could be bought near Lima she would consent to go to it. I then wrote to her cousin at Lima to find out if there were any farms near Lima that could be rented, and soon received an answer that there was no farms to rent. That settled the question of renting a farm. All her neighbors constantly advised her not to move from the farm. I did not say any more concerning it for some time. Presently her two brother-in-laws came to visit us. They said they had been told that there was a large amount of stuff on the farm, such as cattle, sheep, corn, wheat, fodder and hay, but she told them there was scarcely anything. They insisted on my wife telling them just what there was, and she did so, as follows: Two cows, ten bushels of corn, ten bushels of wheat, no oats, twelve shocks of fodder and two and one-half tons of hay. After she had made her report, the two men discussed it, and one told her it ought to be divided, but the other thought not, and the two men came very near quarreling over it. They remained with us for two days and one night, and then returned to their homes without having decided about the division of the farm. A few days after they had been gone my wife remarked to me that now it would be better for us to leave the farm, and we decided to remove to Lima. It was about the middle of January when the brother-in-laws came out to see us. In a short time we began to prepare to move to Lima. After everything had been packed we spent a week in making farewell visits to the neighbors. Everybody was sorry to see us go. On the 28th of February we started for Lima and arrived at our destination the same day.

CHAPTER XX.

For a short time after our arrival in Lima we stopped with one of my wife's sisters, until we could find a suitable house to rent. I soon found one that was located on the same street on which her sister lived. Asking the price of the house the owner said: "Five dollars per month." I paid the money and he gave me the keys. We cleaned the house, moved in our goods, and in a few days were ready for housekeeping. We began at once to attend the A. M. E. church, and took an active part in all the services. In a short time the pastor gave an opportunity to those wishing to join the church to do so, and we united. At that time the church was in a dead and formal condition, and remained in that condition for several years. We were soon the leaders of the church and it did not increase numerically or spiritually until 1875, when the great revival reached Ohio.

The first camp-meeting was held at Landsville, in the State of Pennsylvania, in the year 1868, for the promotion of holiness, and from that meeting the revival of wonderful and complete salvation spread through the State of New York, Pennsylvania, and on west to Ohio and other Western states. The first holiness camp-meeting in Ohio was held at Urbana in the year 1874, and that was a wonderful meeting and from it the revival spread through many counties in Ohio, especially through Hancock, Champaign and Hardin. The first revival in Hancock county was held in September, 1875. The leader of this meeting was Mr. W. Ellis, and several came out into the glorious light of heart purity. In October of the same year another meeting was held in Ramsey chapel, six miles from Dunkirk, Ohio. S. R., the leader, was assisted by W. M. R. Matthews, of Ada, Ohio. In that meeting I heard the first doctrine of entire sanctification. This great blessing I was hungering and thirsting after for six months. I was under deep conviction for a pure heart, and I can truly say that I was not in a backsliding state, for I was walking in the light of justification, as God is in the light, and I was ready to enter into that glorious state of heart purity. Just after noon one day I had arrived from Lima to attend a quarterly meeting. After the business of the quarterly conference was over, Rev.

Clark said to Brother S. S. Rice that he might proceed with the holiness meeting. Brother Rice then opened the meeting by singing the hymn:

Oh! now I see the crimson wave,
    The fountain deep and wide,
My Lord, mighty to save,
    Points to his crimson side.

Chorus.
The cleansing stream I see, I see,
It cleanseth me, it cleanseth me,
O! praise the Lord, it cleanseth me,
It cleanseth me, it cleanseth me.

Brother Rice talked a few moments on how a believer may know whether his sins have been purified or not. Afterward he invited any one who wanted a pure heart to the altar. I was the first one to go forward, for I felt very much in need of a pure heart. Brother Rice was a great teacher. He was so simple in his manner of teaching a soul the way of faith. He was on the inside of the altar. Kneeling before me he asked if I believed the blood of Jesus cleanseth me from all sins now by faith. I could not answer him. He waited for a time and then asked me the same question again. My faith had taken hold of the promises of God, and I said, "I do believe that the blood of Jesus cleanseth from all sin." As soon as the words were out of my mouth I felt as though an electric shock had passed over me. It went through every avenue of my soul, purifying my heart from all sin. There was a voice in my soul saying: "Peace, peace, peace." I was blessed many times. This was the blessing that the apostles received on the day of Pentecost, when they were all filled with the peace that passed all understanding. It was as great a blessing to me as was my first conversion, seven years before. On Monday morning I returned home, where I arrived at eight o'clock in the morning. As I stepped on the porch my wife saw there was a great change in my countenance, and asked: "What is the matter?" I replied that I had received a great blessing. She asked, "What blessing?" That which prepares us for death, I answered, not knowing what else to say. She exclaimed: "Oh, Mack," as she always called me, "that is the very thing I want." I then told her that Brother Clark, the pastor, was going to have the holiness people come to Lima and hold meetings in our church. She asked me when, and I answered, about the 15th of October.

CHAPTER XXI.

♨ ♨ ♨

THE FIRST HOLINESS MEETING IN LIMA.

Brother Rice, of Ada, and Brother E. E. Burlesson, of Cleveland, were leaders of the meeting. A large number of holiness people were in attendance from Cleveland, Berea, and other cities in Ohio, and many came from the State of Indiana. It was a great surprise to the colored people. The pastor announced that there would be a large crowd of people at the meeting, and he wanted as many as could to prepare to take care of some of the visitors. The people came and were surprised that the meeting was to be held in the colored church, and the colored people were surprised to know that all the people who were coming to the meeting were white. But nevertheless, when the people came they were taken care of by the colored people. They were not such as the colored people were wont to call "white trash," but were people of rank. Some were encouraged in the meeting. They were not all old people, but many young men and women were among them.

S. S. Rice was talking on the subject of holiness with my wife at supper one evening. She was under deep conviction, but she did not say very much to Mr. Rice. He asked her to come to the meeting, and she promised to do so. The meeting opened with wondrous power and some few came to the altar that night. My wife was the first to come. The meeting was well attended by numbers from all the churches in the city. Sanctification was preached in that meeting by those who had experimental knowledge of holiness. The meeting lasted ten days. It was a grand meeting. About thirty claimed to have received help and nineteen professed to have received the blessing At the close of the meeting a holiness band was organized in the church and nineteen joined it. My wife was the first one to come out in the experience of heart purity. She did not get the witness of the spirit at that time, but claimed the blessing of a pure heart of faith.

Holiness bands were organized in several cities and towns in Ohio, and in other states. One morning while my wife was busy getting breakfast I was reading aloud from the "Christian Harvester," published at Cleveland, some of the testimonies given in these holiness meetings. One sister said that all the Lord wanted us to do was to fully believe. When my wife heard that statement it came to her with great power. She stepped out of the kitchen into the pantry, threw up her hands and said, "Yes, Lord, I do fully believe." She was filled with the Holy Ghost, and from that day she began to prosper.

The first band meeting was well attended, nearly all the members being present. I was appointed leader of the band. Some were seeking at every meeting. The meetings were held on Tuesday evenings and every Sunday afternoon. It was not long before some of the church members began to find fault, saying that we were having too many meetings. Some opposed the Sunday meetings, claiming to be opposed to keeping the young people in meeting Sunday afternoons. Finally the opposition became so strong against the afternoon meetings that we discontinued them. The opposition kept up until nearly all ceased to attend the meetings, and within a year from the time of the organization of the band there were only six or eight remaining faithful. About that time it looked very dark for the continuation of the meetings. The opposition on the part of some of the church members was so great that my wife said she felt impelled to hold cottage prayer meetings every Friday afternoon. I told her that she had better consult with the pastor. Two or three days afterward she called on him and was told that her plan met with his approval, and he would appoint her the leader. The next Sabbath the pastor gave notice that there would be a prayer meeting on Friday afternoon, and that Sister McCray had been appointed leader. It was her first experience at leading a meeting but she was wonderfully helped by the Lord in her effort at leading. The meetings were thus carried on all summer. Some of the members would say to her: "Sister McCray, it is too warm to have meeting," but she invariably answered them by saying that it is not too warm to die. We still held the Tuesday night band meeting. Sometimes the attendance would be small, but we did not get discouraged. We still called upon the Lord to pour out His spirit on the church The Lord wonderfully answered prayer. In the month of December, 1876, the revival meeting commenced in the church. It lasted three months and was the greatest meeting ever held in Lima. Many people from the country attended the meetings. Some of the hard hearted sinners were converted and the church was in a good spiritual condition for a long time, as a result of that meeting. The church had been heavily in debt for several years, but in one and one-half years after the meeting the church was cleared and was free from debt, and with from $60 to $75 in the treasury. Everything moved along nicely.

56

CHAPTER XXII.

❧ ❧ ❧

OUR HOME IN DAKOTA.

In 1880, 1881, 1882 and 1883 there was a great excitement about our moving to Dakota. Land agents out west were distributing circulars all over the east inviting all old soldiers and sailors to come west and take government land. Soldiers were to have their choice of the land. A nephew of my wife had read one of the circulars. He came to our house and talked to my wife about it. He asked her if I was a soldier, and she said yes. He then said that all soldiers, sailors and old citizens could go out west and take up land. He said: "Perhaps your husband would go out there and take up some of the land. When I came home she told me all about it, and said I had better go and learn something concerning it. She said she would have Johnnie come to the house and tell me all about it and to this I consented. In a day or two Johnnie came and told me all about the matter. After he left I told my wife that I thought it would be very nice to get some land for the boys, but nothing more was said about it for some time. Presently the subject came up again and we discussed it for six months or more before we could arrive at a conclusion. It was the opinion of my wife all the time that I would go. At length I received a bundle of circulars from a land agent at Desmet, Dakota. I took them home and read them carefully. I then asked my wife what she thought about it. She answered that she thought it best to go. We had no choice as to what place to go, so in a few days I wrote a letter to Desmet, addressed to W. E. Whiting, the register of deeds of Kingsbury county. This was in October, 1881. Within three weeks I received a reply from Mr. Whiting, giving a full discription of that part of Dakota. After reading the letter it was fully decided by both that I should go, but my wife did not want me to go alone. I tried to find some one to go along, but was unsuccessful, so on the 12th day of June, 1882, I left Lima and arrived in Desmet on the 14th of the same month. On the 19th I went out and selected 160 acres and sent in my papers to the land office at Watertown. I soon received my title to the land and hired a man to break ten acres for me, in compliance with the homestead laws. I also built a shanty and made it my home all that summer. During the first week in October I started back to Ohio. I stopped a few days in Chicago and arrived in Lima on the 17th of the month.

For the first five months of my stay in Dakota I had no intention of moving there, but I was delighted with the country, and told my wife that we should sell out and remove there. My wife said it was not best to sell our property, but I insisted that it was not best to leave our property in Lima unsold. Nothing more was said for some time, but the subject came up again, and after discussion we decided to sell. Our eldest son was in Vernon, Mich., and we wrote to him that we were going to move to Dakota. He answered us and said that we had better not move. We wrote again, saying that we wished to see him before we started, and he came at once. My wife said that if Ed would only go with us everything would be all right. When Ed arrived he saw that we were getting ready to move, and asked us if that was our intention. His mother answered that it was, and added that it was desired that he go with us. After a few days of meditation he consented to go. Then I began to hunt some one to buy our property. Soon a man was found who offered me $1,200 for it, but something happened and made it impossible for him to get the money, and eventually I sold the property to another person for $1,000 cash. The deed was made out, the money paid and everything settled. This was in January, 1883. I began to buy stock, such as horses, hogs, cattle and chickens, and a wagon. We had enough to fill a car. Another family by the name of Williams was preparing to go with us. We went to the P. F. W. & C. Railroad company to see about getting two cars from the Chicago & Northwestern railroad, and they were forwarded to Lima at once. On Monday morning, April 9, 1883, we commenced to load our goods into the cars. We left for Dakota with one of the cars and Mr. Williams the other. We left our families at home until we reached Desmet. We were nine days on the road. At some point in Wisconsin we were delayed three days by reason of the roads being blockaded with trains of immigrants bound for Dakota from all parts of the United States, especially the eastern and northeastern states. We arrived in Desmet on the ninth day of May, with all our stock in good condition. We wrote for our families to come, and moved on our lands just as soon as we got temporary stables built for our cattle. Our families arrived and we had most of our goods on the farms. Mr. Williams' family arrived several days before my wife and children, as the latter stopped in Chicago for several days to visit relatives.

CHAPTER XXIII.

❧ ❧ ❧

OUR HOME IN DAKOTA.

Our first son was a barber by trade, so he stopped in Des-met and started a barber shop. Our farm was twelve miles from the same town, and it was very lonely with only three of us in the family. Our little boy was ten years old and had no playmates and no school to attend. The neighbors were few and scattering. As for my wife and I, we had no church to go to, no prayer or Sunday school to attend. We did not know any Christian people in the neighborhood. They had no thought for the Sabbath and hunted and fished as on any other day. They seemed to have left their God in their old home bac kEast. But in the name of our God we erected our family altar night and morning, and looked to our God to find help to tell the story of the cross in our prairie home. Wife thought there must be some way to have meetings some place, and I told her that when we became acquainted with some of the neighbors we would find out if there were any Christians among them. The next day when I came to the house for din-ner wife said that she had had a visitor that morning. I asked her if it was a man or woman and she answered that it was a man. She said that while she was at work in the garden she

looked up and saw a man coming and waited to see if he would
stop at our house. He was singing a hymn, and my wife said
to herself that he must be a Christian. He came to the garden
and said good morning, and asked how we liked the country.
My wife answered, very well, if we could only get acquainted.
He said, that's so. After they had talked for half an hour he
said that his errand was to borrow a hoe, if we had one. She
let him have it and before he left he asked us to come and
visit with them. He said that his name was Currier. My wife
told him we should call to see them in a short time. We called
and found him to be a Christian. His wife at one time had
also been a Christian, but had backslidden. He had two married sons living on adjoining farms. The elder son was not a
Christian, but the wife of the younger son was a Christian
woman. There were about nine children in the three families,
aged from two to sixteen years. We had a good visit with
them. The summer passed very pleasantly but our hearts
were pained to see the wickedness among the people. The fall
work began and the neighbors were very kind to help us. When
the fall work was over there was nothing to do but to feed the
stock, and wife suggested that we go to Mr. Currier's and see if we
could not hold prayer meeting at his house. I agreed with her
suggestion and we made arrangements to go the next day. Mr.
Currier was well pleased with the idea and said he would go
and invite Mr. Morris and family. On Tuesday afternoon the
first meeting was held, with the members of four families in
attendance. The meeting, the first one in that neighborhood,
was held in January, 1884, and was a blessed one. In the four
families represented in the meeting five persons were Christians, three women and two men. At the close of the meeting

we made arrangements to have another at the home of Mr. Moore on the following Tuesday evening at the same hour. In this way the meeting was carried on till the latter part of February, and all of us were greatly strengthened. Mr. Moore, who had been a Christian, but had backslidden, was reclaimed in the meeting, but did not stand true very long, as he fell back into sin again when the meetings closed about the first of March, when spring work commenced.

The first week in March was too stormy to commence the sowing of seed for the wheat crop. One morning after my little boy and myself had finished feeding the stock and milking the cows, we were all seated and talking over various affairs, when Prince said: "Mamma, I wish there was a house somewhere in which school might be held." The directors of the township had said we might have school if we would furnish a house to hold it in and find some one that could teach according to the law. No school houses had at that time been built in that part of the country. Neither of us answered him for a moment, when wife said that she believed Mr. Hance Lee would let the people have his house to hold school in. There were three Norwegians, brothers, who lived next to us, their farms joining ours on the north and south. The brothers all lived in one house and the shanties on the other two claims were vacant. Prince said he would go over and ask Mr. Hance about using his house as a school, and his mother told him to go. In a few moments he was back with the information that the house could be had to hold school in. The next morning the two brothers passed our house. I asked Mr. Hance about the house and he said they might use it if there was any money in it. Wife thought it would be well to go to speak to Mr.

Currier about the house and I went. He was very glad at the prospects and said he would go and talk with the directors about it. Those officials said it was all right, but there was no money for rent, so it would be impossible to get a teacher.. The next thing to do was to find some one qualified to teach. There was no single woman in the neighborhood, and only one married woman that could teach. She was the mother of two children, one aged four and the other two years. She was one of Mr. Currier's daughters-in-law. They hardly knew how to arrange it, but at last she told Mrs. Currier that if she would take care of her children she would pay her for it. To this arrangement Mrs. Currier assented. Mr. Currier took Mary down to the superintendent where she passed the examination and received a legal certificate, to the joy and gladness of all concerned. This was the first public school in that part of the country. It commenced March 1st, 1884, and closed the first of July of the same year.

CHAPTER XXIV.

SUNDAY SCHOOL.

In April we conceived the plan of having a Sunday school some place in the neighborhood, and wife suggested that some one might be found to open up their house for the school. We talked the matter over with Mr. Currier's family. Then the word was given out to all of the neighbors and all were in favor of the Sunday school. Then the question arose, who will open their house for it. At that time there was but one house in the neighborhood large enough, and that was ours. Mr. Currier suggested to some of the neighbors that Mr. Mc-Cray's house was the best place in which to hold the school, as it was the largest. Then a discussion arose in regard to the matter and some said they would not go if the Sunday school was held in the house of a colored person. Others said that made no difference and many pleasant things were said. The Bible says that we must bear all things for Christ's sake and not to find fault. Sinners and formal church members have crucified Christ, as he has died for us. We had learned to suffer all things for his name's sake. The subject of organizing a Sunday school came to a standstill in the neighborhood. Opposition of this kind is what hindered the progress of the black race in America for nearly two hundred years. They were, and are now, hindered in every way because their faces are black. The people in that neighborhood thought to hold Sunday school in the house of a colored person was giving too much honor to the race. It was the first Sunday school in that part of the country. Many not only failed to come themselves, but did all in their power to keep others away. But the people did not know that the Lord had something to do with having a Sunday school in that part of the country. We did not want Sunday school held in our house, our only object was to carry forward the work of the Lord, as He showed it to us.

By this time the news had reached all through the neighborhood, and some people living southeast of us came to see about it. Mr. Currier happened to be at our house at the same time, and arrangements were made to organize the school at our home. The next Sunday, according to arrangements made then, the school was duly organized. The question again arose, whose house shall we have the school in? Mrs. Booth said many had objections to coming to Mr. McCray's to Sunday school, but as for her family there was none whatever. Mr. Cluett said the same thing. I said that I did not think it wise to have the school at our house, but for the present it would be better to hold it at Mr. Booth's, as their rooms are just as large as ours. A vote was taken and carried to have it at Mr. Booth's. The first session was held in their home, five miles south of our neighborhood, on the 18th of May, 1884. The school was carried on successfully during the entire summer. The most of the attendance was from the neighborhood. That was the Lord's way, not ours, and we gladly accepted it. "The way of the Lord is not our way." By having the Sunday school at Mr. Booth's we were greatly blessed also in having preaching every two weeks by a preacher from Desmet. The school closed on the 15th of October, as the cold weather set in the 10th or 15th of November.

CHAPTER XXV.

ℐ ℐ ℐ

BUILDING PUBLIC HOUSES AND PLACES OF WORSHIP.

When school stopped the people were greatly agitated for six months. It was decided that each township should submit propositions to the voters to build as many school houses as were needed, at a cost of $700 each. The usual time for spring election was on the second Monday in March, and the nominating conventions were held one month earlier. Notice was given that the conventions would be on the tenth day of February, for the purpose of nominating the different officers. I went to the convention and found most all the voters in the township present. There was great discussion in regard to the school house proposition. Some of the voters were not in favor of building school houses at all. Others thought each district should build its own house at a cost of $300 each, and others were not in favor of holding religious meetings in the school houses. One man said that for himself he did not believe in religion, but he would not want his family to live in a neighborhood where there were no religious meetings held. The excitement run very high and the convention was called to a close by the chairman. They proceeded in the nomination of officers. The balloting commenced, all the officers were placed in nomination, and the convention was over. Between the convention and the election, a space of one month; those who op-

posed the building of the school houses did all in their power
to influence voters against the proposition. The election day
was on the sixth of March, and every voter was requested to be
at the polls to vote. The forenoon was very blustery, but I
went, and after I had voted remained about an hour to find out
about the votes cast in the morning. Several others remained
also. One man said that from the best information he could
gain all the votes cast were against the school house proposition, and I believed such to be the case. I returned home
down-hearted and discouraged, and as soon as I got into the
house my wife asked, "Well, Mack, how is the election?" I
replied that I was discouraged, and believed we would be defeated on the school house proposition. All the Christian
people were in favor of the building of school houses.
My wife said: "I have been praying all morning for the
proposition to carry, and I know the Lord will answer
my prayer." I told her that most all the men who had
voted in the morning had cast their ballots against it,
but she answered that there would be enough votes
cast in the afternoon to carry the proposition. We did not
say any more about it. The next morning Mr. Currier came
along and in answer to our question said that the school house
proposition had carried by a small majority. My wife said:
"I told you that." The school question was now settled, and
the county officials soon gave notice to the township officials
that there would be seven school houses built in the township
at once, and they were to be finished by the first of November,
so as to be ready for the winter term of school. The school
houses were planned, let to contrators at a cost at $700 each,
and were finished according to the contract.

CHAPTER XXVI.

❧ ❧ ❧

THE SUNDAY SCHOOL QUESTION.

The question of Sunday schools came up in our neighborhood again. My wife said that Mr. Lee would allow the use of his house for Sunday school purposes. The winter term of school would be out the last of March and then the school house would be vacant. I went to see Mr. Lee about the house and he said he had no objections to people using his house in which to hold Sunday school. Nothing more was said about the matter until about the first of May, when my wife suggested that we see Mr. Currier about the Sunday school. I was nearly through putting in my spring crops. The next week I went to Mr. Currier and told him about Mr. Lee's house. He thought there would not be much trouble in organizing the Sunday school, as several more families had moved into the neighborhood since the spring of 1884. After we had talked the matter over we decided to have all the people meet at Mr. Lee's house on the second Sunday in May. Mr. Currier agreed to tell as many as he could see and we did the same, and also sent word to others. Within a week the entire neighborhood had been notified, and on the day appointed for the meeting there were from twelve to fifteen families present. A motion was made that Mr. Currier preside over the meeting. Mr. Alcock was elected superintendent, Mr. Grant Barton secretary, and Mr. Currier treasurer. Three teachers were also selected. The school progressed from Sabbath to Sabbath, with more new scholars at each session. They kept coming until the little house was too small. Something had to be done to make room. All agreed that the house was too small, and that it was too hot to stand outside. This was about the first of July. After the Sunday school had closed we went home, and then my wife said that perhaps we could get a tent, or some muslin to make one out of. We went to see Mr. and Mrs. Currier to get their advice in the matter. They were going to Desmet the next day, and I said that probably my wife could go along with them. They said they would be glad to have her go. I went home and told my wife of the arrangement, and she said she would go. When they came along the next day my wife was ready. They inquired about a tent, but could find none. My wife said to Mrs. Currier that they would go to Mr. Morris' store and see about getting some muslin. As they entered the store Mr. Morris spoke to my wife, as he was acquainted with us. They asked to see some cloth suitable for making a tent, and he said the best thing he had was some unbleached muslin, one and a half yards wide, which he thought would be just the thing for tenting. The ladies said they would take two bolts. My wife said to Mr. Morris that they had no money to pay for it with, and he answered, "I can charge it, Mrs. McCray." To this she said all right. Their next trip was to get four or five pieces of lumber twelve to fourteen feet long, which they procured from a lumber yard they passed when on the way home. By Sunday the tent was ready to put up, and then there was plenty of room for all. The school proved to be a great blessing to the neighborhood. Many gave up their Sunday work in order to be present at the school. Most of those who attended were Methodists, and some one said that as so many were attending the Sunday school it would be nice to get a preacher to come out and preach to the people every two weeks. The proposition was talked over by several, and one man said he was going to Desmet the next week and he would see if he could find a minister that would come out and preach every second Sunday. At the close of Sunday school the superintendent announced that there would be preaching immediately after the Sunday school and invited all who could to stay. Nearly all remained. The minister was there three times. After he had finished his discourse he asked all those who were Christians to let the fact be known, and going through the audience he found that most all those present belonged to some church. He announced that he had found out that most all the people were Methodists, and that if the people had no objections he would form a class, and then they could have a class or prayer meeting every Sunday after the close of Sunday school. After the Sunday school closed the people accepted the offer to have prayer and class meeting. The minister was a Methodist, and appointed leaders. The Sunday school, class and prayer meetings were continued all summer, but only a few attended and so the meeting and Sunday school closed October 15, 1885.

CHAPTER XXVII.

⚜ ⚜ ⚜

The school houses were now built and and we could hold meetings in them. Presently the words came to my wife, just as distinctly as if a man had spoken them to her, and she said: "I know it is the Lord that has called me to work, and I must do it." I tried to convince her that it was her own thoughts, but she said no, that it was the voice of the Lord speaking to her. I opposed her at first, but she did not say very much. She was a wise woman in the things of the Lord, and knew the call of the Lord better than I did, as she had received the call before leaving Lima. The enemy, who has something with which to oppose every one who is called of the Lord to work for the salvation of souls, tested her on every side. Her greatest trial was that she had no education, and the enemy struck her several hard blows by telling her that it would be impossible for her to call sinners to repentance when she could neither read nor write. The test was a hard one to overcome, but the Lord was a present help in the time of need, and she called on Him for aid. One day she was praying to the Lord about not having an education, when words came to her saying, "You lead the people as I lead you." She answered, "Yes, Lord, I will," and arose from her knees with the victory in her soul. It is better to follow the Lord wherever He may lead you. The

Lord soon showed me that I did wrong in opposing her in the work. The school houses were all numbered and named from the farms on which they were located. I asked her one day in which building she would hold her first meeting, and she answered in Mr. Currier's school house, which was numbered six. It was situated just one mile from our home. I also asked her how soon she would begin, and she replied: " Just as soon as we can give notice to the people." She also asked me to go to Mr. Currier's and tell them to send the word to all the neighbors north of us. We could spread the news in the other direction.

The first meeting was held on the evening of January 5th, 1886. Not very many were present at the first meeting. It was the first time that my wife had come before the people as a preacher. The meeting was opened by singing the hymn:

> There is a fountain filled with blood,
>   Drawn from Emanuel's veins,
> And sinners plunged beneath the flood,
>   Lose all their guilty stains.

I had to lead the singing but the people did not help very much at first. It was arranged after prayer that Mr. Currier was to read a lesson. After this the speaker took for her text the third verse of the eighteenth chapter of Matthew, which reads as follows: "Verily I say unto you, unless ye be converted and become as little children ye cannot enter the Kingdow of Heaven." She was wonderfully helped by the Lord to preach the truth to the people. At the close of the meeting she asked if there were any who desired to seek the Lord and one or two answered yes. Several prayers were then offered and the meeting was dismissed. She announced that there would be meeting every night. It continued every night with an increased attendance. On the third two or three came to the altar, and at the end of the week five had been converted. By the middle of the second week the school house was nearly filled, and the third week it was crowded. Many who did not understand how a woman who was not educated could preach the gospel came merely to witness the excitement. Mr. Alcock, who was the best scholar in the neighborhood, said it was a wonder to him; that he had never before seen a person who could 'preach without being educated. One one old man, a Southerner, said he did not have much love for the colored people, but he became greatly agitated over the meeting and said he would not attend because the niggers were at the head of it. About two weeks before the meeting began he rebuked Mr. Currier for helping on with it, and also for keeping company with us. He said he did not propose to keep company with niggers. He had at one time been a class leader in a Methodist church. Wife and I heard of it but kept our counsels in regard to the matter. About the middle of the third week two of the boys of the old Southerner came to the altar and that brought him to the meeting. That night there was not standing room in the house. After wife had finished preaching she called for seekers to come forward to the altar, and the same ones came forward. The third one had promised the night before to come also, but for fear of his father, refrained from so doing. The audience was filled with seekers. Wife went back through the audience talking to the people. Presently she saw the old Southerner, Lloyd by name, and said to him: "Mr. Lloyd, please go forward and help the laborers with their work." He refused to go and when wife pressed him for his reasons for not going he said he would rather not give them.

The meeting continued for three weeks, closing on Sunday night at the end of the third week. About fifteen souls were converted during the meeting, nearly all of them married people. Among the converts were two or three young boys. At the close of the service it was announced that there would be meetings the following Sunday morning and evening. On the Monday morning after the close of the revival meeting wife said to me: "Mack, I want to go to Mr. Lloyd's this morning." I asked her reasons, and she said in regard to the trouble he had had with our eldest son in regard to a land deal. Mr. Lloyd had purchased 160 acres from our son, and claimed that he had been cheated out of $75, and thought that we should return it to him. Wife said that while she was praying the Lord impressed it upon her heart that we should go to Mr. Lloyd and arrange the matter. I agreed to go. She then wanted me to drive past Mr. Currier's, as she wished him to go with us. I drove to Mr. Currier's house, but did not get out of the wagon. Wife told him that she would like to have him go over to Mr. Lloyd's with us, as we wished him to be present during the settlement of some business matters.

He said he would go. He went to the house for his hat and overcoat and in a moment was ready. We drove to Mr. Lloyd's house. He met us at the door and invited us in. He assisted us in putting the horse in the barn, and after we had returned to the house and were all seated, my wife told him that we had come over to find out what his objections were for not coming to the altar a few evenings since to pray with the other seekers.

She told him if there was any fault on her part that she would try to make it right. In answer Mr. Lloyd said that so far as going forward to pray for seekers he was not in the proper condition. He then said: "Your son cheated me out of seventy-five dollars and I think you ought to pay it." I reminded him that at the time the trade was made he knew my son was of age and in business for himself, and that when he bought the land he said nothing to us about it. My wife said that she did not think it right for us to pay the money when we had nothing to do with making the deal. Mr. Lloyd answered that parents should help their children to make their wrongs right if possible. I then said we would pay him if we were only able, and he said he would be satisfied with fifty dollars. My wife said that we had no money, but that our son had gone east and as soon as we heard from him we would write and ask him to help us raise the money, and it would be paid as soon as we could secure enough money. Mr. Currier asked if that was satisfactory, and Mr. Lloyd answered that it was. My wife then said that we would have a word of prayer before going home. We all kneeled down and my wife offered a special prayer for Mr. Lloyd and his family. After we had arisen from our knees we began to make preparations to go home, but Mr. Lloyd said we must have dinner before we started, as it was then about noon. His wife was a cripple, but she soon had dinner ready, and we partook of the bounties of Mr. Lloyd, who had said only two weeks before that he did not intend to associate with niggers.

After dinner we returned home, when my wife remarked that she was well blessed in her visit to Mr. Lloyd's. I said that I was very glad we went. She answered that she was very thankful to know that the Lord always makes men do the very things they do not wish to. After that Mr. Lloyd had no objections to associating with colored people, and when the meetings were held in the school house a good audience was always in attendance, and Mr. Lloyd and most of his family were there at all the sessions. Soon arrangements were made to have regular services in the school house every Sunday and prayer meeting on Thursday evening.

CHAPTER XXVIII.

❦ ❦ ❦

The place of holding the meetings was afterwards changed to the Bartrum school house, which was three miles north of our farm. There was a large class of Methodists in that neighborhood. The meetings and Sunday school were well attended all through the summer and fall of 1886. After Christmas it was decided to hold a revival service. The meetings were held for one week, and then it was thought best to procure a preacher. At the close of the meeting several ladies were standing together talking, when one turned to my wife and said: "Mrs. McCray, what do you think about having a preacher?" My wife said that if acceptable, she would lead the meetings. They all looked at each other in surprise and one said: "Mrs. McCray, you help us all right, but we think it best to have a preacher. My wife answered that she would do the preaching for them, and they said nothing more. These women were the leaders in the church, and one of them, Mrs. Prath, was the wife of the leader of the class to which my wife belonged. On their way home they stopped at Mr. Barthune's house, which we all had to pass on the way home. Here they held counsel as to what had better be done about a preacher. My wife came up for discussion, and one said, "Mrs. McCray is a good Christian woman, but she is colored and I do not think it best for us to accept her offer to lead the meeting." Another suggested that as Mr. Prath was class leader it would be best for him to take charge of the meeting until a preacher could be secured. This course was decided upon and Mr. Prath prepared to take charge of the meeting to be held the next Monday evening.

The evening arrived and the house was crowded. After singing and prayer Mr. Prath stepped into the pulpit and announced that as a minister could not be secured to lead the meeting, the duty fell upon him. He promised to do the best he could and asked all Christians to pray for him. His sermon, which was nothing more than such an essay as a school boy would compose, written on paper. After talking about five minutes, he began to read his essay. When about half through he became mixed up, which caused some of the young people in the audience to laugh. This confused him so that he at once called upon some one to pray. The sermon was a complete failure. His condition was like that of many who go forth to call sinners to repentance. They are nothing more than dead, formal church members, who know nothing of the saving power of God. Sometimes the Lord stops them in their blindness, for we read in His holy word that if the blind lead the blind they shall both fall into the ditch. The meeting continued for several nights, but Mr. Prath did not attempt to go into the pulpit to speak again. The meeting closed with the last of the week. The people wanted to choose their own leader, and therefore, no one was lifted out of their dark and sinful state.

CHAPTER XXIX.

LOST IN A SNOW STORM.

About the middle of February, 1886, after our son Prince had gone to school, I had finished my chores and gone into the house. I asked my wife if she would like to go over to Mr. John Hackett's, as it was such a nice morning. She said that she did not care to go then, but I answered that if we did not go I did not know when we would have a chance again. After thinking for a time she said that she did not care to go. I told her that I was going, but did not like to go alone, and with this went out to the barn. In a few moments I returned to the house and found that she had decided to go along. I told her to get ready while I hitched the horses and in a few moments we were on our way. Mr. Hackett lived just one mile southeast of our farm, and our horses had soon covered the distance. As we drove up Mr. Hackett came to the door and invited us in. My wife went into the house while Mr. Hackett assisted me in unhitching the horses and putting them in the barn. Going to the house we had a very pleasant visit for an hour and a half, when I remarked that it was time for us to go home. Mrs. Hackett insisted that we have dinner before we returned and began at once to prepare the meal, and in a few moments we were all seated around the table. Just as we were finishing dinner, Mr. Hackett's brother, who lived only about twenty rods away, entered the house. As he opened the door we could see that it was storming. Mr. Hackett asked his brother if it was much of a storm and he answered that it was, and rapidly growing worse. He also said that it had been storming about an hour. We had not noticed it as the windows were iced over from the steam of the cooking. I went out to see how the storm was and found it very bad and growing worse. We immediately made preparations to go home. I soon had the horses hitched to the sleigh and driving up to the house my wife took a seat beside me. There was plenty of straw in the bottom of the sleigh and we had three or four blankets. Mr. Hackett asked if I thought we would have any trouble in getting home. I told him that I did not anticipate any trouble, as the tracks made by the sleigh when we came over were yet visible. We bade them goodbye, and started the horses off just as fast as they could go.

It was one o'clock in the afternoon when we started, and before we had gone far we discovered that we were in a terrible storm. Soon we lost sight of the sleigh tracks. For a time we kept on as we supposed straight ahead, but at last I stopped the horses, and said to my wife that we were lost. She thought not. The heavy storm and black clouds made it so dark that we could scarcely see each other sitting as close as we were. My wife then suggested that the horses be started and allowed to take their own way. After we had thus wandered around for some time I said that I did not think we were far from home, but she thought we were three or four miles away. Again the horses were allowed to take their own course, but after they had walked for some time I stopped them and getting out of the sleigh walked a few steps ahead of the horses and found a place where the snow had been blown away and the ground left bare. It was where some one had cut hay, and I thought I could recognize it. I climbed into the sleigh and started the horses. They were soon plunging through a terrible big snow drift which they finally pulled through and were again on the level plain. Then I stopped them again, and said the Lord would have to deliver us from this storm. Wife said she was praying for deliverance. I started the horses again. Soon the clouds began to break and I could see some distance ahead of the horses. Thinking I saw some weeds I started the horses toward them. The horses plunged into a snow drift again and soon were in the road where the wind had cleared away the snow. As soon as the horses were in the road they turned and went south, and had only gone a short distance when I saw the top of a house. I said I believed it was our house, and wife told me to drive up and we could get shelter, even if it was not our own home. Arriving at the house we found that my predictions were correct. Oh! what a wonderful time of rejoicing over our deliverance from the storm. One of wife's hands was frozen very badly. We did not see our little boy

Prince for three days. The third day he came home unharmed, so we gave God the glory for his wonderful help in the time of trouble.

CHAPTER XXX.

❧ ❧ ❧

THE ORGANIZATION OF A FREE METHODIST CLASS.

My wife became convinced that she was led by the Lord to organize her work into a body. I asked her what she would call it and she said she did not know until she had seen Mr. Currier. He said he would not join any body except the Free Methodists. We did not know anything about this denomination, but Mr. Currier had been converted at a Free Methodist camp-meeting about three years before he came to Dakota. He had formerly been a member of the Advents for over thirty years, but after his conversion at the camp-meeting he did not fellowship with them any more, though he did not join any other organized body. His wife, who had also been converted about a year later at a Free Methodist camp-meeting, wanted to join that church but did not do so because Mr. Currier would not join. Mr. Currier said that he considered the Free Methodists the best, as they did not admit members into church fellowship until they were converted. They also taught holiness, and that the members should live pure and holy in the present world. Wife said that was just the kind of a class she wished to see organized and asked us to take a paper around and ascertain the number that were willing to join such an organization. We found six, but as Mr. Currier did not decide to join we let the matter rest for a time. Several days later Mr. Currier was a caller at our home, and the subject of the class came up again. After considerable solicitation on the part of my wife he decided to put his name down as one of the members. This made seven on the roll, three men and four women. Mr. Currier then said he would send to McCook county for a Free Methodist minister to come and organize the class. He also wrote to Elder J. B. Freeland, chairman of the Iowa and South Dakota conference of the Free Methodist church. Within two weeks he received an answer from Mr. Freeland, stating that he would visit us on the first of April. He came and was a guest at our home. He asked if it was the intention to organize a Free Methodist class, and my wife answered that she had been led to organize the work into a body. He then said that he did not know whether we could stand the rules of the Free Methodist church or not, as they were very straight. Wife asked him if they were any straighter than the Bible. He said no, but that all churches did not hold their members to Bible truths, as theirs did.

Saturday night Mr. Freeland preached in the school house. Sunday morning at ten o'clock he preached again. A large crowd was present to hear him. He spoke with the power of the Holy Ghost. And our souls were fed the bread of life. After the sermon was ended a short speaking meeting was held, after which he called those who wished to join the class forward.

He then asked if we had the witness that our sins were forgiven, and all answered yes. His next question was, "Have you received the blessing of a pure heart since you were converted?" Some answered that they had and others that they had not. He then asked if they were seeking it, and all answered yes. He said that all members of the class must give up tobacco, ruffles, laces, ribbons, tucks, flowers, feathers, neckties, silks, plug hats, and all kinds of secret societies, strong drinks, gold and costly apparel.

Wife and I had not received any teaching upon plain dress so our clothes were very fashionable and worldly for the use of holy people. Wife had to take several of her dresses to pieces and to remove the trimming from others, but by so doing she gained one or two dresses. Our hearts were prepared to receive the whole truth, and also to walk in the light that may shine in our pathway. The Bible does not say anything about fine clothes but it does say that we should not adorn our bodies with gold or costly apparel. The writer knows from a blessed experience that every one that hears the Holy Ghost teaching on fashionable and worldly dress cannot become converted until they are willing to give up their fine and fashionable dress. The class was organized with Mr. John as leader. Wife received license to preach April 15th, 1886.

CHAPTER XXXI.

※ ※ ※

MEETING AT THE HALVERSON SCHOOL HOUSE

Wife decided to hold meetings at the Halverson school house, and on Sunday had the Sunday school superintendent announce that a meeting would be held there on the following Monday evening. On the opening night a good crowd was in attendance. The greater number of people in that neighborhood were Norwegians and Swedes. The meeting opened with singing, after which Mr. Currier read a short lesson from Luke's gospel. Wife took her text from the lesson read and had much liberty and freedom in talking to the people. It was a good meeting. At the close she announced that there would be meeting every night and all were invited to attend, and also to tell their neighbors. The attendance increased every night. Soon wife asked that a mourner's bench might be prepared, but Mr. Currier hesitated somewhat and asked her if she thought there would be need of one. She said she thought there would.

The first night there was a little excitement in the back part of the room. It was occasioned by a Norwegian who was under deep conviction, but who did not know how to express himself. So he broke out into loud laughter. After my wife was through preaching she went back to talk to him, but could not make him understand. However, he kept on laughing. The meeting continued all that week. On Saturday and Sunday nights there was not seeking room in the house. Sunday night after my wife was through preaching she gave everyone an opportunity to speak. A great many took part, and a large number were under deep conviction, but did not come forward to the altar. One woman and the Norwegian who laughed so loud were converted. My wife announced that she was undecided as to whether the meeting should be held longer or not, but announced that one would be held the next evening, when it would be announced whether they would continue or not. After the audience was dismissed two or three young men were talking concerning the happenings of the evening, when one spoke to an elderly man, named Durkey, standing near, and said: "Mr. Durkey, they hit you pretty hard in the speaking meeting to-night." Mr. Durkey inquired as to what was said and they told him various persons had spoken in regard to the old men being converted. Such was the case, but there were several old men in the meeting and the remarks had been made in a general way and with reference to one in particular. However, it angered Mr. Durkey and he said he would stop the meeting those niggers were running. The next morning he saddled his horse and rode around to all the voters living in that school district to get them to sign a protest against holding the meeting in the school house. He said we were burning the oil that had been procured for use by the school, and through his persuasion most of the voters in the district signed the protest prepared by him. He then went to the director and wanted the key, but the director told him he was in the wrong and would not let him have the key. Mr. Durkey insisted, however, that he would lock up the school house after school was out. The director warned him that he should not do so, but he went at once to the school house and arrived there just as school was out and the children were fixing the fire ready for the evening meeting. Taking the key from the children he ordered them out of the building, put the chairs, table and benches out on the platform, then locked the door and put the key in his pocket.

That evening my wife said that she wished to go to the school house early, so we started about half-past five o'clock. She stopped at Mr. Halverson's, while I went over to the school house to get everything in readiness for the meeting. Noticing the furniture outside the door and several children standing near I asked what it meant. They answered that Mr. Durkey had put them there but they did not know why he did so, except that he did not want meetings held there any more. I asked if Mr. Durkey had gone home, and they said he had gone to Mr. Halverson's. Going to Mr. Halverson's I found Mr. Durkey and asked him why he had locked the school house door. He said that he did not intend for us to hold any more meetings there and expose him before all the people. I asked how we had exposed him, and he said by telling him he was an old man and ought to be converted. After expostulating with him for some time and finding he was firm in his decision that there should be no meeting I told him he would at some time be sorry for his action. We at once began to make preparations to return home. On our way we met several loads of people coming and informed them that there would be no meeting and told the reason why. All were very sorry. Mr.

Halverson said a few days afterward that a large crowd came, some from eight or nine miles distant, and all condemned the action of Mr. Durkey very much. He would not have locked the school house door had he remembered the good book says: "Whosoever shall offend one of these little ones that believe in me, it were better that a mill stone be hanged about his neck." The interruption of the meeting was the talk of the entire neighborhood for several weeks.

About three weeks later, about six o'clock one evening, a stranger passed our house. He was a very rough looking man and was poorly dressed. He did not stop at our house but went to the next neighbor's and begged bread, until he came to Mr. Durkey's house, which was the fourth one from ours. There they gave him his supper and he went on his way rejoicing. After supper Mr. Durkey finished his work and after reading for a time retired to his bed. He had safely locked his barn and left everything in good shape. Between twelve and one o'clock he was awakened by a strange noise, and going to to the door saw that his barn was all in flames. When he and his men reached the barn it was so far gone that nothing was saved except one horse, and it was burned so badly that afterward it had to be shot. The family decided that the stranger had fired the barn but he was never heard of again. Next morning people came from many miles around to see the ruins Mr. Durkey confessed that he had done wrong in stopping the meeting and all the people agreed with him. Afterward his wife separated from him, his son left home, and he was left all alone in his trouble. He believed that this had come upon him because he had stopped the meeting. His whole family was broken up and he lost everything he had. His farm was sold and he came very near being killed with a horse so he had a bitter experience in trying to interfere with the work of the Lord.

CHAPTER XXXII.

❧ ❧ ❧

LEAVING THE FARM.

In 1885 and 1886 we lost part of our crops by drouth and early frost. In 1887 we put in a larger crop than we had ever done before. We put in ninety acres of wheat, corn, flax and oats. Harvesting commenced on the first of July. We had cut our oats and five acres of wheat. The balance of the wheat was not ready to cut and would not be for four or five days. In the meantime a friend who had no binder asked us to come over and cut his wheat and in return he would help harvest ours when it was ready. We talked the matter over and concluded that I could go over and cut for him for two or three days at least, and as our crop was very large his help in return would serve us well. I went and was at his place three days and nights. On the third day there came a heavy hail storm. Our crop was directly in its path and was nearly all destroyed. The following morning when I went home my wife met me and said that she had been all over the farm and that there was but little of the crops left. I told her that I did not know what we should do as this was the third crop to be destroyed. I went over the fields and it was a sorrowful sight to see such a fine crop of wheat almost entirely whipped out by the storm. I cut and cared for what was standing and from the wheat, oats and all got about three hundred bushels. Our corn was nearly all destroyed and our garden crops were almost pounded into the ground by the hail.

We submitted to it without a murmur or complaint. We figured our debts and found they amounted to seven hundred dollars, most all of which fell due that fall. What to do we did not know, as we had no grain for seed and but very little for bread, and could not borrow any more money. We did all our fall plowing for the spring crops, but said little about our troubles. One day in the latter part of October I was on my way to Bancroft, a little town on the railroad about one and a half miles from our farm, for the purpose of having my plow sharpened, when an impression came to me that I must move to Huron, where our oldest son was barbering. Huron was thirty miles south of our farm, and the county seat of Beadle county. It is located on the James river and at that time had a population of about 3,100. After returning home I told wife what had come to me and that the best thing we could do would be to go to Huron. She asked if it was the intention to sell the farm, and I told her that I had thought nothing about that. She said she did not see how we could leave the farm without selling it. I told her we would consider the matter and do what we thought best for us. I talked with several of the neighbors and all said we had better not leave the farm. One day while in the county seat I asked a friend

of ours about the matter and he said we had better borrow seed
and keep our farm. I told him we could borrow no grain as
we had no money with which to procure other grain to pay
it back. When I returned home I told wife I thought it best
to sell everything on the farm except our house and furniture.
She wished time to think the matter over. In a few days Mr.
Currier came to our house and among other things told my
wife that she would regret the day we left the farm. In a day
or two afterwards she told me what Mr. Currier had said, but
I told her I could see no way out of our difficulty, except to
sell off our goods. She then said that I could do just as I
thought best, but that she wanted to retain one horse and a
cow. We then decided to leave the farm and move to Huron.
On the 15th of February, 1888, I had the bills printed for a
public sale, to be held on the 7th of March. The day of the
sale was a fair one and a large crowd was in attendance. The
sale commenced at ten o'clock in the morning and by three
o'clock in the afternoon everything had been sold. After our
debts had been paid we had nothing left but our household
goods. In ten days after the sale all business matters had been
arranged and on the 17th of March, 1888, we arrived in Huron
and stopped with our married son for a few days before going
to housekeeping.

CHAPTER XXXIII.

❧ ❧ ❧

OUR HOME IN HURON.

There were six churches in the city, but Christianity was nothing but a form. As we were members of the Free Methodist church we did not confine ourselves to any one of the churches in the city but attended all. In the city we found one or two colored families and eight or nine single persons. My wife determined at length to ask Mrs. McDonald if we might not have prayer meeting at her house, and she said she would be very glad to have us to do so. She sent word to all the colored people and the meeting was held during the first week in April. Afterwards we held several prayer meetings at the same place. Mrs. McDonald's husband was an old man, about sixty-five or seventy years of age, and very wicked. He was converted in one of our meetings. Others were under deep conviction, but did not yield. Mrs. McDonald professed to be a Christian, but she did not know anything about practical Godliness She was much worse than the younger people in worldly form. Her husband died a year and a half after his conversion.

We held the prayer meeting only a short time, as they were soon tired of attending regularly. We then attended the class meeting at the Methodist church, which was held every Sunday morning. Only a few of the older members attended the class, and there was no life nor power in it, only dead form. I attended the Sunday school, until a string band was brought in to make music. Then it became a place for entertainment of pride, and a show. This only serves to blind the minds of the young, so that they do not know the true object of the Sunday school. It is very sad indeed to witness how far the present generation is drifting away from the simple method of teaching to the children the way of eternal life. There is very little hope for improvement in teaching when the teachers themselves know very little or nothing about the way of eternal life, either by experience or mental knowledge. They can not impart that of which they have no knowledge themselves. The Sunday school of this present time has become so worldly that the children think of it only as a place to go to be amused and show their fine clothes.

The first revival meeting we attended in the Methodist church was conducted by a young Evangelist whose home was in Canada. H. H. Dresser was pastor of the church. The young Evangelist was limited in educational attainments, but after his conversion he had been called to preach. He led the meetings two or three evenings, when the official members of the church became very much displeased with him. The officials were the well to do persons in the church, and it did not please them to be told that they must be converted. They complained to the pastor, saying that the Evangelist did not come up to their ideas, and that it was for the best interests of the church to close the meeting. This did not meet with the approval of the pastor, who desired to give the young man further trial, but the officers insisted that the meetings close. The pastor knew that the persons who objected to the meetings were the ones who contributed most liberally to the support of the church, and, regretfully, he closed the meeting. The Evangelist was given his pay, and allowed to go to other fields where his work was more acceptable, and no souls were saved that winter.

In the fall of 1889 the conference sent Rev. H. H. Dresser back to the church for the third successive year. Soon after the holidays had passed the pastor called the official board of the church together to make arrangements to hold revival meetings. It was arranged that the meetings should be held by the pastor himself, with the aid of the presiding elder and ministers from other churches. The first meeting was held the middle of January and there were meetings for three or four weeks. Several ministers and the presiding elder came, but could do no good, as the members were nearly all dead spiritually. The ministers themselves had little of the power of God upon them, and therefore could not wake many of the members from their careless condition. The meetings closed. One old man, who had been a backslider for thirty or forty years, was reclaimed. He joined the church without having been converted. So the best two years of Rev. Dresser's pastorate was a failure, so far as the salvation of souls is concerned. What was the cause of his failure? The answer is that, like most of the preachers of the present day, he was preaching without the power of the Holy Ghost and with a desire to please the rich church members. It is very sad, indeed, to see Christian churches drifting into this state, but, nevertheless, it is true, and every true man and woman must admit it to be a fact.

The word of God says, "In the last days they shall wax worse and worse deceiving and being deceived." But our dear Lord has always had a few in all ages that would not defile themselves with sin, thanks be unto our Lord, who giveth us the victory over the world, the flesh and the devil, through our Lord and Savior Jesus Christ.

In the fall of 1890 conference sent a new minister to the church. His name was F. G. Newhouse. He was heartily received by all the members, and proved himself a better preacher than the former pastor. In the early part of November he called the official board together to counsel in regard to holding a revival meeting. The officers told him it would be impossible to have a meeting at that time, as the whole city was in a gambling scheme to have the state capital located there. At the election held soon afterward the city lost the capital, and with it two hundred thousand dollars that had been put into the gambling scheme. As most all the rich church members were interested financially in the scheme they were very sore and in no condition to go into a revival meeting, and the pastor was very sorry that it was impossible for him to carry on a meeting in which poor sinners might find their Savior. John Wesley, the founder of Methodism, said it is not best to make the rich man a necessity, but churches should be built large and plain. Now, however, churches are constructed on the most expensive plans. This necessitates a large revenue and concessions are made to the rich in order to induce them to join, and thus secure their monetary support. The result is that soon everything is in their hands, and the church and pastor are controlled to suit their selfish interests. There is no time to work for the salvation of souls until the new church is paid for, and then it becomes a place for parade and show. The older members, who once enjoyed the life and power of God in their souls, now are compelled to sit and look on. This pride and show has become so popular that many of the older members believe that this new order of things is all right. What a sad condition the mass of the church members have fallen into. There is no hope for many of them.

In 1891 the rich members of the church became reconciled to the loss of the capital, and in January consented to allow the pastor to have a revival service. The services of Mrs. Dennis, an evangelist of Goshen, Ind., was secured for three weeks. She came and the meeting began at once. She was a good preacher and the church was crowded every night. She preached very strongly on the subject of conversion, and deeply impressed many of the church members. Several asked what it meant to be converted. One evening she preached on the subject of conversion, and before her talk was ended many of the members found that they had never been converted. She also held several meetings for the special purpose of preaching on the subject of holiness. In these meetings very few received any benefit, as few understood anything about conversion. The meeting closed, and the pastor stated that one hundred and twenty-five had professed conversion. Nearly all of them united with the church. Oh! how sad to see these poor souls so deceived, knowing nothing about being born again. The blood of the people will be required at the hands of the watchman who does not warn them faithfully.

CHAPTER XXXIV

❧ ❧ ❧

OUR HOME IN LIMA AGAIN.

Huron failed in her efforts to be created the capital of the State of South Dakota, and this caused a large exodus of its citizens to other places. Had Huron secured the capital there would have been a great boom, but failing in this, great disappointment was caused. As we had lost everything, we concluded to move elsewhere, but could not decide as to our future location. My wife had two sisters living and did not wish to move further away from them. I was undecided as to where we should go, but both of us were determined to leave Huron. Several days later I wrote to a friend in West Superior, a real estate man who had gone there from Huron. He knew the line of work I followed and wrote that West Superior was an advantageous point for me. We talked the matter over several times, and at last I proposed that my wife and Prince should go to their old home in Ohio, while I would go to West Superior and have a home ready for them in the fall, at which time they should join me. While my wife thought the arrangement a very good one, yet she did not assent to it, but said she would consider it. A few days later, while I was walking along the streets of Huron, the thought came rushing

into my mind as loud and clear as though some one had spoken
to me, that Lima was the best place for me to go to. I did not
tell my thoughts to my wife for several days, but it kept
recurring to my mind all the time. At length I told wife about
it. Her first inquiry was as to where the money would come
from to enable us to make the trip. I answered that the Lord
would open the way for me to earn the money. This was in
February. Wife said very little to me about it, as she did not
want to make Lima her home again. She prayed over the matter for several days, and at length became reconciled to the
fact that it was the will of the Lord that we should move back
to Lima. Afterward she told me that the Lord made it very
plain to her, revealing just what we were to do. While in
prayer she was told that our mission was to go back to Lima
and establish there the real work of Bible holiness, as a second
work of grace received in the heart of every one after their conversion. This had not been taught in Lima for six or seven
years. When we moved west in 1888 we left two bands of
holiness people, one in the Trinity M. E. church and the other
in the A. M. E. church. The former was held at the home of
Mrs. Hart, but after her death it ceased to meet, and the latter
also had disbanded. The subject of holiness, so far as organized bands were concerned, had ceased to be taught in Lima.

We at once began the preparations for moving, selling a
great share of our household goods. By the second week in
April we were ready to make the start, and on the fifteenth
day of that month we were on our way back to Ohio. We
stopped and visited with an old friend for about two weeks and
arrived in Lima the latter part of the month.

CHAPTER XXXV.

⚜ ⚜ ⚜

LIMA AGAIN OUR HOME.

We arrived in Lima via the C. & E. railroad on the 29th of April, 1891. During our eight years of absence we found that many changes had taken place. The oil industry had increased the population, and instead of the village we had left we found a city. We were made to feel very sad that Christianity had fallen into such a low state. We attended the A. M. E. church, with which we had formerly been connected, the first Sunday after our arrival, and were very much surprised to see the small congregation at the morning service. After preaching, class meeting was held, but we soon saw that the strong power that had reigned supreme formerly had been blotted out. We attended this church all summer, excepting during three weeks when we were visiting in Kentucky, Louisville and Goshen, the former being the place where my wife was born and raised.

After an absence of thirty years she had an opportunity of seeing once more the log house in which she was born. We walked about the plantation and saw many places where she played in her childhood days. We went down to the old graveyard where her only brother and two of her sisters were buried, and also visited the grave of her former mistress. The old plantation had not been worked for many years and had grown up into bushes and weeds. We found a number of the old fruit trees, still bearing, and gathered a few peaches and pears to take home with us. We met some of the old residents, who were living the same as in days of old. Some who had been children with her, and many of her relatives were yet living in the neighborhood.

Our visit to Kentucky was a very pleasant one indeed. The boat in which we made the trip from Cincinnati to Louisville was one of the largest that traversed the Ohio river. The ride was a delightful one. We had the privilege of eating two meals on the boat, supper and breakfast. The state room in which we spent the night was nicely furnished. The thirty years that had elapsed since my wife came on a boat to Cincinnati had wrought a great change. Then colored people were not allowed in the cabin, but were compelled to sleep among the horses and cattle. Only as servants to white passengers were they allowed to enter the cabin. That spirit has not yet all passed away but is more noticeable in some places than others. After visiting for three weeks we started for home over the same route we had taken in coming. We left Louisville at 3 o'clock in the afternoon, but owing to a heavy peach crop and numberless stops to take the fruit on board, we were five hours late in arriving at Cincinnati. From there we took the C. H. & D. railroad for Lima, where we arrived at 8:30 a. m.

We had been stopping with Mrs. A. Byrd, my wife's sister, but in a few days we moved into a new house on South Baxter street, and in a short time were housekeeping again.

My wife then suggested that it would be well to hold a few cottage prayer meetings. I heartily approved of her plan, as so few attended the regular prayer meetings at the church. The first meeting was held at our house, and only a few were there. The next meeting was held at her sisters and no one came. Then one was held on Spring street, with the same result. On our return home from this meeting my wife asked me what I thought of it. I answered that the people did not care for praying, nor did they care to attend a meeting appointed for prayer. We finally gave up cottage prayer meetings, but regularly attended those held at the church. These were gradually losing all interest. The pastor would open the doors of the church for members every Sunday, but we thought it best not to join. At length I decided to have a talk with the pastor on the subject of holiness, which was our theme with all men, for without holiness of heart no man shall see the Lord. One Sunday afternoon I spent a few hours with the pastor discussing different subjects in the Bible. He did not know anything about holiness, as experience meant knowledge. He believed that a person would grow better and better, and just before death the Lord would make them holy. The word of God says: "I am not the God of the dead, but of the living." According to this, then, all the blessings that God has promised to men are in the present time. They do not mean to-morrow, or the next day, nor just before we die, but to-day. The word says: "Behold this day is the day of salvation." If any man hears the voice of God calling him to repentance the heart should not be hardened, as it may be the last call. Finally, I said to the pastor that I would not join the church just then, but would wait on the Lord. He thought that the best thing to do, and nothing more was said. We continued attending the church until the fall of 1891.

CHAPTER XXXVI.

✄ ✄ ✄

THE ORGANIZATION OF THE FIRST HOLINESS MEETING IN LIMA,
OHIO.

One day in November, while we were talking about the
spiritual condition of the city, wife proposed that a letter be
written to Brother Thomas K. Doty, of Cleveland, inviting
him to come or send some one to hold a series of meetings outside of any church. Mr. Doty was editor of the Christian
Harvester, published at Cleveland, and a personal friend of
ours. The invitation was sent and in reply he told us to write
to Rev. Hiram Archers, of Big Pines, Ohio. We did so and he
sent us Testimony Stewart, of Bellefontaine, her son Elmer,
Mrs. Dunmire, of Bucyrus, and W. E. Williams, of Versailles,
O. Mrs. Stewart was leader of the meetings. The rest came
as assistants. Our first meeting was held November 15, 1892,
in the teacher's examination room in the court house. As this
was too noisy a place we only met there a few times. A room
in the old street car barn which had been arranged for mission
work was then occupied. The members of the mission only
allowed us to meet there one night. The next place of meeting was in an old vacant house on West Spring street, which
was very much torn up. The owner agreed to rent it to us for

five dollars a month, and we accepted the offer. We had no money to pay the first month's rent, neither had we enough to furnish it with heat and light. We did not know what to do. We knew that the Lord had led us thus far, and we also knew that it was the will of the Lord that the meetings should continue until His whole truth was established in this city.

As all four of the workers were stopping at my house, I went to my work the following morning with a heavy burden on my heart concerning the work. About eight o'clock Mr. Williams, one of the workers, came to me and asked if I was well known in the city. I answered that I was. He then suggested that it would be a good idea to take a subscription paper around among the business men and ask them to assist in carrying on the work of the Lord. I told him that I did not care to write up such a paper, so he agreed to do it, with the understanding that myself and wife should sign it. When I returned home in the evening he had the paper ready, and the next day, Friday, I started out with it. I was undecided as to whom I should approach first, but finally decided that the man for whom I was working was the proper person. I handed him the paper. He kindly read it over, approved of it, and handed me a dollar to start with. By the evening of the following day we had money enough to supply all our needs, and on Saturday evening had our first meeting in our church. We continued until the latter part of January, 1893, and at the close seven of us organized ourselves into a holiness band. We held regular services on Sunday, and prayer meeting on Wednesday evening. We were instructed to send to J. S. Robinson, of Union City, Ind., and ask him to take charge of the work. It was stated that he would be a great help to us, as he was preaching in the independent holiness line, and had been for many years. As we were just starting out in that line we were very much in need of a helper. In answer to our request he said he would come and hold a ten day's meeting for us. The date of his arrival was fixed for March 10th. At the close of these meetings there was some talk of buying a lot and building a church. We inquired into the matter and were told that if we were organized into a body, according to the laws of the state, we would be better prepared to buy real estate. We then held a special meeting to organize ourselves into a church. After some discussion as to a name, it was decided to call it the First Holiness church of Lima, Ohio. This action was taken on the 11th day of April, 1892. The church was known by this name until the evening of the 9th of April, 1895, when it was thought best to change the name, and a meeting was called to take action. On motion the name, "First Holiness Church of Lima" was dropped and in its place was substituted by proper action "The Mission Church of Christ." For some the place of meeting had been in an old frame house on West High street, but after the adoption of the new name we rented Stamet's hall for our regular place of worship.

In the name of the Lord we went forth in this city to do the very best we could in advancing the practical truths of the religion of the Bible. It must be confessed that our efforts have been weak indeed, but knowing no better we could do no better. Many things have hindered us from accomplishing all that we desired to do. Without education, very few in numbers and poor in worldly goods, and without influence among the masses of the church going people, they were not attracted to our meetings, and thus our opportunity for doing good has been limited. In olden times the people had leaders who taught in the temples, instructing their hearers in the various forms and ceremonies. But when Jesus came into the temple and found them buying and selling he turned over their money tables and drove them out, on account of which they were ready to stone Him and all His disciples. When we look back upon what we have accomplished in our little work, which seems very little in the sight of men, we are reminded that the Lord has said: "To him that is faithful until death I will give a crown of life." We are conscious of the fact that we are working for the salvation of immortal souls in the manner that the Lord would have us.

CHAPTER XXXVII.

✻ ✻ ✻

SHE FEELS THAT HER HUMAN LIFE IS NEAR AN END.

About noon on the 15th of June, 1894, the subject of this sketch was taken very sick. When I arrived home for dinner she said to me that her work was done, and that she was going to die. She asked that the children be sent for. Our elder son and his family were living in Wisconsin and our younger son was at Wilberforce College. I told her that she was alarmed at her condition and that she was not so sick as she thought.

But no argument of mine changed her opinion. I ate my dinner and returned to my work, feeling very sad. As time passed by she continued to grow worse, although she was able to do her work and attend the meetings all summer. About the middle of September she had grown so weak that she was unable to do the heavier household duties, and a month later was unable to do any work whatever. She was, however, able to be up every day.

On the 24th of November I received a letter from C. S. Hanley, editor of the "Fire Brand," a religious paper published at Shenandoah, Page county, Iowa. We were close friends to him and his wife and had assisted them in conducting a training home and school for missionaries, and also in the publication of the paper by donating money and such other help as we were able to give. He wrote that they were about to start to New York with a band of missionaries, who were on their way to Africa. I succeeded in having them stop at Dayton, Ohio, and hold meetings. We went to that city to be present at the meetings, arriving on Wednesday, November 20. The meeting was to begin the following Saturday. We met Brother Hanley and his wife and the missionaries. The meetings were very enjoyable. There were eight missionaries, all young men, the youngest being a boy of sixteen years. They had given up father, mother, sister, brother and friends and all comforts of home, that they might go to heathen lands to save poor souls. Two of them had been born in India. They were sent to this country by their father, after the death of their mother, in order that they might be trained for missionaries. They had been in the training school in Shenandoah for two or three years and were now on their way home to India to pend their lives in missionary work. Surely the harvest fields is great and the laborers few. Oh! may the Lord of the harvest send forth more laborers into fields already ripened for the harvest.

We spent two days and one night in Dayton and then returned home. My wife did not get any better, though she was not confined to her bed until the day before she died. The night before her death she was very sick and in the morning her condition was alarming. I was at her bedside all the morning. About ten o'clock she said to me: "Mack, are you not going to take me up." I answered, "No." She then added: "It is so very dark to-day." About 11 o'clock she said to those about her: "I thank you all for your kindness. I am so sleepy and will now go to sleep." We left the room and I said to Mrs. Fenwick, the nurse, that I would go and do some work that was awaiting me. Giving directions where to find me and instructions to send for me at once if any change for the worse took place, I left the house. I had been gone only fifteen or twenty minutes when she aroused and said: "Where's Mack? He has not gone to work, has he?" She asked Mrs. Fenwick and some other ladies who were present to assist her into a chair. She was in the chair only a few moments when she called for a drink of water. She said: "Oh? how sweet it is to trust in Jesus." The minister came in and said a few words to her and then sang a hymn. She joined in the singing and her voice was as strong as ever. The minister left the room, but his wife remained. About one o'clock the sufferer bowed her head. The minister's wife went to her side, lifted her head, and found that the spirit had taken its flight.

Mrs. Fenwick at once sent for me, but I arrived too late.

She had passed away from this world to the heavenly kingdom prepared for her from the foundation of the world. I can truly say that during her entire life almost, she had taken hold on eternal life and had fought the good fight of faith. And henceforth there is laid up for her a crown of life by Him who has said: "Be thou faithful unto death and I will give thee a crown of life." She is gone forever to join the blood-washed throng who have passed up through great tribulation, and whose robes have been washed and made white as snow in the blood of the Lamb.

ADDENDA.

❧ ❧ ❧

THE TRAINING OF CHILDREN.

This chapter has been written after much reflection and prayer, yet the writer has never offered anything to the public with such a deep sense of his inability to accomplish the work according to his wishes. Never has he been more inclined to accuse himself of presumption, in attempting a task beyond his strength. In submitting this chapter to mothers a few words of explanation might be given as to the object in writing it. The desire has been to give a little counsel to mothers in various situations, such as a confidential friend might impart, with full knowledge of all the circumstances and bold enough to speak the truth. Mothers should know many things that are not touched on in sermons or in a general way, but which affect the conduct of multitudes. The solemn warnings given in the scriptures are not adhered to as they should be, either by parents or children. The word of God says: "Train up a child in the way he should go and when he is old he will not depart from it." In these days of hurry and rush few parents take the time to properly train their children. They fail, in that they do not start in time to instruct the children in the things they should know, and which would be of everlasting benefit to them through time and eternity.

Some one asked how old a daughter should be before her mother begins to instruct her. The answer is given: Twenty years before the child is born. In explanation of this answer it is only necessary to state that a mother should be well instructed in order that she may impart the same to her daughter. She should spend much time in instructing her children, so much so that she should never allow them to keep any secrets from her. The mother should be able in all actions of her children to show them the right and wrong. There are many things the girls should know before they go out into society. If the mothers do not tell them at the proper time, they will learn it from some one who is probably not careful to instruct them in the right and wrong. The writer wishes to impress upon mothers the necessity of telling their daughters everything that they should know. Should they do this they will never be compelled to look back with sorrow and grief because they failed to give such instruction as would keep them in the path of purity and righteousness.

Boys should be taught to live as pure a life as the girls. Much disgrace, as well as crime and sin is committed among all classes of people, both rich and poor, high and low. Possibly only a portion of these will come to shame in the eyes of men, but all must some time stand before the judge of all the earth to give an account of their deeds, whether they be good or evil. We live in such a fast age that very few mothers take time to tell their children concerning eternal things, which would save them many times from sin and disgrace. The great responsibility rests upon the mothers, and they need a great deal of wisdom in order that they may give their children the best advice. In order to give such advice there must be praying mothers. Then should her children depart from the way in which she has led them the blame rests not upon her, since she has done her whole duty. The Bible states that they will not depart from the way.

The writer humbly hopes that every mother who may chance to read these few lines will take great pains in trying to follow the advice given. Although the writer is only one in the common walks of life, yet he has great sympathy with mothers who are training children for this life and that to come. Some mothers spend most of their time preparing their children for this world. That is all right so far as it goes, but the preparations for the world to come should come first. If that is neglected all is lost. The word says: "What shall it profit a man if he gain the whole world and lose his own soul." Great trouble and sorrow come to many mothers because they do not begin in time to restrain their children from having their own way. Every child, as soon as it can talk, should be taught to mind. Children should always understand that when the mother says anything she means it. Some mothers will allow themselves to be forced to consent to disobedience on the part of the child by protracted crying and screaming. This is all wrong. Should a mother permit such actions a few times, ever afterward the child will know exactly how to proceed in gaining its wishes. When too late, the mother will see her mistake.

Beware, mothers! A hint to the wise is sufficient. In these last days there are but few praying mothers. They do everything else but pray. There are but few children that have heard their mother pray for them. Some go through a form of prayer, but do not know of the mighty power of God that saves a soul from all sin. The Bible says all are born in sin, and it is safe to add that most all children are brought up in sin and die in sin. Their blood will cry out against the parents in the soon-coming judgment. O! mothers, be wise and seek the Lord with your whole heart, that you may be converted, so as to pray for your children. There is not much preaching done these days, under the power of the Holy Ghost, that will arouse men and women out of their sleep in sin, so that they may see their lost condition and that their children are lost with them. Children in these days know the Bible salvation, if their parents belong to the church, and many of them think that they must join the church too. So, therefore they all drift along unawakened to the terrible wrath of God, which will come upon all that are not converted and saved from their sins.

Now, let the parents do their duty toward the children. Then they will not need to look back in regret and see wherein they have failed in giving proper training. And let the children do their duty toward their parents in all things, that their days may be long upon the earth.

A FEW THOUGHTS ON MARRIAGE.

✤ ✤ ✤

It is in the mind of the writer to write a few words on the subject of marriage, setting forth the cause for so many unhappy marriages. In the first place, in this day young people do not take long enough to consider this holy union before entering into it. When a young man begins to think of getting married he does not stop to think of anything except to get a wife, and most all girls act in a similar manner. The Bible says: "He that findeth himself a wife findeth a good thing and obtains the favor of God." Prov. 18: 22; 31: 10, 11, 12. Read also Ephesians 5: 25-28. There are so many things that should be carefully considered before entering into the marriage relation. The first thing the prospective wife should do is to consider that the marriage union is a holy one, and, second, that it should continue until death shall part them. If these points were carefully considered before marriage, in connection with a few others, there would be few, if any, divorces. Third, the temper and habits of each should be carefully studied. If a man is very quick tempered and marries a woman of similar nature they will never live happily together, especially if the man takes a drink of whisky occasionally. If the woman finds out before their marriage that the man drinks she had better break the engagement. If she does not, she might just as well put a rattlesnake into her bosom and say that it would not bite her as to think of living happily with a man that will drink.

Some women will say: "Oh, I will make him promise me that he will quit drinking before I will marry him." He tells her that he will never drink any more, and she believes it will be all right to marry him. Then they prepare for the wedding. The present looks very bright indeed and the future seems full of roses. Many that see the newly married couple think they can never have any trouble. Everything goes along all right for a time, but trouble will come sooner or later to that home, as it does to every home. One sorrow passes, only to give place to another and another until the man and wife scarcely know what to do. The husband, who has promised that he would never drink any more, forgets his promise and takes to drinking, under the impression that it will assist him in bearing the sorrows of himself and his family. One drink calls for another and soon he begins to neglect his family. The wife, seeing that he has broken his promise, is at her wit's end, scarcely knowing what to do. Some of her friends will advise her not to live with him. She applies for a divorce, and the court will grant it, according to law.

I would advise a woman, if she knows a man drinks before she marries him, not to marry him. The Bible says that the woman which hath a husband is bound by the law to him so long as he sinneth, but if he be dead she is loosed from him. Read Romans 7:2, 3. In the present age men have become so blind in sin and lust that they do not regard the law of God, but push onward in a mad rush to have their sinful appetites and fashions satisfied. Virtue and purity are almost unknown.

Men and women think it all right to have three or four living husbands and wives, because the popular ministers of to-day do not cry out against the awful sin of adultery, and the people go on in all kinds of sin and crime without fear of God's judgment, which He will in due time pour out upon the ungodly men and women.

Most young boys and girls before they are old enough to go out in company, talk among themselves about their beaus or sweethearts. Many mothers engage in this kind of talk with their children, and in this way the subject of marriage is so common among the boys and girls before they are of age. Many girls are married at the age of fourteen or fifteen and boys at seventeen or eighteen years. Many at the age of twenty-five or thirty have had two or three husbands or wives. They do not think of the great duty and care marriage should place upon them. The most they think of is to have a good happy time, but instead of a happy time they have trouble, sorrow and dissatisfaction. The result is everything except what they expected.

Some marry for one thing and some for another. The writer asked a certain young lady why she wished to marry a certain young man. She answered that I may have a home, and added: "I think he will be good to me." The writer said: "Suppose he has no home to take you to, what will you do then?" She could give no answer, although she was past twenty-five years of age. She had engaged herself to him without any consideration for the future. No doubt most young people marry that way, especially among the common people. The rich are more careful in their marriages, but will have their troubles also, though they man be able to hide them from the public. A young lady will marry a young man because he is pretty and dresses well; another because the young man has a good position; another because his father or mother has an abundance of money. Or a young man may desire to marry a young lady for similar reasons. Marriages with such motives as these cannot fail to be unhappy. The Bible says he who builds his house on a sandy foundation shall lose all when the storms and troubles of life come.

To such marriages troubles are sure to come. Sometimes everything is lost in wild speculations, sometimes through dishonesty, or by sickness and death. Sometimes a man will murder his wife or a woman her husband. Sometimes husbands will run off with other men's wives, or wives with other women's husbands. When such trials as these come into the family, who then is able to bear all the distress. No family is able to withstand such trials unless supported by the grace of God. This is not much thought of by the young people of to-day. All they think of is to have a good and happy time. Oh! what a sad mistake all are making who expect to have a happy time in this life without the grace of God in their soul.

Oh! that the young and old would stop and think before they go farther. All the things in this world cannot make one truly happy, for true happiness does not consist in the things of this world. Men may have plenty of money, and possess banks, farms, railroads, horses, fine homes, carriages, cattle, and, in fact, everything the world calls good, and yet they cannot build their hopes of happiness on any of these, for they will all perish. Thousands and thousands of families have all these and everything that the heart could wish for, and yet there is no true happiness in these homes without the religion of the Lord Jesus Christ. There is something in the soul of man that all the things of this world cannot satisfy without true religion.

Oh! how strange and sad it is that the human heart seeks happiness in every way before turning to true happiness, which is the love of God in the soul. The Bible says: "Seek first the kingdom of heaven and its righteousness and all things else shall be added unto you." It does seem that all the endeavors of mankind are lost in a mad rush to seek the pleasures of this world and have a good time. The Bible says: "This world and all its pleasures shall pass away, but he that doeth the will of God abides forever and forever." Oh! old men, old women, young men, young women, boys, girls, will you be wise and choose eternal life rather than to enjoy the sinful pleasures of this life for a short season?

Yours truly,   S. J. McCRAY.

THE END.

www.ingramcontent.com/pod-product-compliance
Lightning Source LLC
Chambersburg PA
CBHW020800020726
47495CB00008B/2516